Vanished into Plein Air

Books by Paula Darnell

DIY Diva Mystery Series

Death by Association

Death by Design

Death by Proxy

A Fine Art Mystery Series

Artistic License to Kill

Vanished into Plein Air

Hemlock for the Holidays

Historical Mystery

The Six-Week Solution

Vanished into Plein Air

PAULA DARNELL

CR

Campbell and Rogers Press
Las Vegas

CR

Campbell and Rogers Press

Library of Congress Control Number: 2020920353
ISBN: 978-1-887402-20-0

Publisher's Cataloging-in-Publication Data
provided by Five Rainbows Cataloging Services

Names: Darnell, Paula, author.
Title: Vanished into plein air / Paula Darnell.
Description: Las Vegas : Campbell and Rogers Press, 2021. | Series: A fine art mystery, bk. 2.
Identifiers: LCCN 2020920353 (print) | ISBN 978-1-887402-20-0 (paperback) | ISBN 978-1-887402-21-7 (hardcover) | ISBN 978-1-887402-19-4 (ebook)
Subjects: LCSH: Murder—Fiction. | Artists—Fiction. | Art—Fiction. | Women—Fiction. | Arizona—Fiction. | Mystery fiction. | BISAC: FICTION / Mystery & Detective / Amateur Sleuth. | FICTION / Mystery & Detective / Cozy / Crafts. | FICTION / Mystery & Detective / Cozy / Cats & Dogs. | GSAFD: Mystery fiction.
Classification: LCC PS3604.A7478 V36 2021 (print) | LCC PS3604.A7478 (ebook) | DDC 813/.6—dc23.

Cover design by Nicole Hutton of Cover Shot Creations
Formatting by Polgarus Studio

First Edition

Published by Campbell and Rogers Press
www.campbellandrogerspress.com

*Dedicated, with appreciation,
to cozy mystery readers everywhere*

Chapter 1

"Look at the crowd, Emma! Brooks made such a big deal that he was inviting only a few people to the private pre-opening of his new gallery, but it seems like half the town is here."

"Sure does," my daughter agreed. "Do you think they'll serve champagne?"

"I'm sure there'll be plenty. Now that you're twenty-one, you're entitled," I said. with a wan smile.

My daughter and I had celebrated our respective birthdays a couple of weeks earlier, just days apart. Unfortunately, I'd now hit the mid-century mark, and I wasn't too thrilled about it.

"Are you OK, Mom?"

"Oh, sure. Just thinking about that zero in my age now. It makes me feel so old."

"Honestly, Mom, you look way younger than fifty. You look like you're forty—really you do."

"That's always good to hear."

A year ago, my daughter wouldn't have been able to say the same. I'd still been in shock after my husband unexpectedly divorced me and married his twenty-five-year-old assistant, who was only a few years older than Emma.

What a difference a year made. I'd moved to a new town in a new state, turned my part-time art hobby into a full-time business, and bought the house, with its own attached art studio, that I'd rented when I'd first moved to Lonesome Valley, Arizona, from Kansas City.

"Hey, beautiful! You didn't tell me you were coming to the opening."

I turned to see Chip, a young artist who flirted with me every time he saw me, although he was only a few years older than Emma.

"Hi, Chip," I said, ignoring the compliment. I'd learned that it was best not to take his flirtatious ways too seriously. "Did Susan come with you?"

"She's right over there." He pointed to a boutique a few doors down from the gallery.

I spotted her checking out the shop's window display. When she looked our way, she waved and hurried over.

"Lonesome Valley Resort's mall is really something," she said after we exchanged a hug. "I don't know why I've never shopped here before. I'm surprised Brooks didn't move his gallery sooner."

"I guess he's turning over a whole new leaf. He has a year's worth of shows by other artists already scheduled, from what I understand, but none for himself."

"Sounds like a smart move to me. His artwork's not very good, to put it kindly."

"What a crush," I said as we slowly made our way toward the door of the new Brooks Miller Gallery.

"Mom, they're having people show their invitations at the door to get in."

"I have mine in my bag. Good thing I remembered to bring

it," I said, pulling the elegant, gold-trimmed card from my purse.

"Aunt Susan?" Chip asked.

"I have mine, too."

"Well, I didn't bring my invitation, but I can be your plus one, I suppose," Chip said.

"Sure, that'll work. It looks like most of the crowd is here to listen to the string quartet," Susan observed, pointing to a group of musicians who were setting up in front of the gallery.

Susan and I handed our invitations to the young woman who greeted us at the door, and we filed in. We'd been invited to a "private pre-opening showing of paintings by world-renown artist Ulysses Durand," and, evidently "private" meant just that.

Although we'd left the crowd behind outside, we could hear the quartet tuning up before they began playing a sprightly number. Brooks, who managed the Lonesome Valley Resort, owned by his family trust, had undoubtedly arranged for the musicians.

Ulysses Durand's paintings reminded me of Ralph Anderson's, with their precise details and sweeping views of Western landscapes. Ralph, now in his mid-eighties, had been one of the founders of the Roadrunner Gallery, an artists' cooperative on Main Street I'd joined a few months after my arrival in town. That's where I'd met Susan, Chip, Ralph, and lots of other members artists, and the gallery had become my home away from home.

"How about some champagne, Auntie?" Chip offered.

"Don't call me Auntie," Susan said automatically, for all the good it would do her to object, since Chip never tired of teasing her. "And, yes, I'd love some."

"Amanda?"

"Sure. Thanks, Chip."

Chip was about to head toward the bar set up in a corner of the gallery when Emma asked, "Aren't you going to offer to bring me champagne?"

"Sorry, Emma. Are you sure you're old enough to handle it?"

"Very funny."

"Don't mind Chip, Emma," Susan advised. "He's always kidding around."

"I noticed."

Just then, a distinguished-looking man, impeccably dressed in a suit and tie, entered the gallery, and Brooks, looking equally distinguished in his own bespoke attire, rushed over to greet him. When I heard Brooks call the man "senator," I nudged Susan. "Isn't that Senator Hastings?" I asked her.

"It sure is," she confirmed. "I guess we're in good company."

We gathered in front of a large oil painting of the Grand Canyon, so that we'd be out of the way. While Susan and I examined the brushwork, Emma surveyed the guests.

"Mom, Anne Robinson and Terry Snyder are here," she said excitedly.

"Who?"

"You really don't know?"

"No clue."

"They're *only* the hottest new Hollywood power couple ever. Oh, I can't believe it!"

"Believe what, Emma?" Chip asked as he returned with four glasses of champagne neatly arranged on a silver tray.

When Emma told him, his eyes widened.

"I'm impressed," he muttered as he stared at the movie stars. "Looks like Brooks pulled out all the stops."

Chip held out the tray, and after we'd each taken a glass, he offered a toast to the Roadrunner.

"To the Roadrunner!" we said in unison as we clinked glasses.

"Another celebrity," Chip said, motioning toward the door where Brooks was greeting a lanky man who towered over his petite wife. In her sparkling red, sequined cocktail dress, she was garnering as much attention as her husband.

"Is he a basketball player?" Susan asked Chip.

"Is he! He's the star of the Phoenix Suns."

"I wonder how Brooks was able to entice the celebrities to attend," Susan said, "but, I guess if you have enough money, anything's possible."

"He probably comped them suites for the weekend here at the resort," Chip guessed. "But where's the star of the show? We haven't seen Ulysses Durand yet."

"Probably around the corner in the back room," I surmised. Like the Roadrunner, Brooks's new gallery had a free-standing wall in the center, which partially divided the space, providing more display areas for paintings.

"Shall we?" Chip asked. "I'd like to meet him."

Susan and I agreed, but Emma hung back.

"Later, Mom? I'm going to try to talk to Anne and Terry. Maybe I can take a selfie with them."

"OK, Emma. Good luck!"

Chip, Susan, and I rounded the corner into the back room of the gallery, where several people had gathered around the famous artist. There didn't appear to be an opening to join the group, so we bided our time by looking at the paintings until Ulysses Durand left his admirers and began making his way around the room, greeting guests as he went. We held our ground and as soon as he came to us, we quickly introduced ourselves and let him know how much we enjoyed his artwork.

"It's great to have some other artists here," Ulysses said genially. He was a short man of about sixty with gray hair who wouldn't normally stand out in a crowd. "I know a couple of local artists. I hope they'll be here tonight."

He looked past us and broke into a smile.

"Here's one of them now. Please excuse me."

We turned to see our friend Ralph leaning heavily on a cane.

"His arthritis must really be bothering him," Susan said. "I've never seen him use a cane before."

We were surprised when Ulysses embraced the old man. Ralph didn't seem quite as enthusiastic in his greeting as Ulysses had been, but that wasn't unusual since Ralph tended to be reserved.

The two stood in front of the largest painting in the room, discussing it, until a new group of guests came into the back space, and Ulysses moved on to talk to them.

Ralph spotted us and motioned us to come over

"Sorry. I don't mean to be rude," he apologized, "but my knee's killing me today."

"Let me find you a chair," Chip offered. "There must be one around here somewhere."

"No, no," Ralph protested. "I don't want to be a nuisance. I'm all right standing here. Funny thing is the knee wasn't even bothering me yesterday. Unfortunately, it would have to kick up a storm today."

"Aren't you scheduled to work in the gallery tomorrow?" Susan asked. "I can fill in for you, if you like."

"I just may take you up on that. Can I let you know in the morning?"

"Sure. No problem."

I was glad that Susan had volunteered because I couldn't. Tomorrow Emma would be returning to college in Southern California, and we were planning on leaving for Sky Harbor Airport in Phoenix at nine in the morning, the same time the gallery would be opening for the day.

"I take it you know Ulysses Durand," Chip said to Ralph.

"Yes. I do. Thirty years ago, he was my star student."

Chapter 2

No wonder their artwork looks so similar, I thought. I could see Ralph's influence in every brushstroke on Ulysses's painting. Yet, fame-wise, the student had surpassed his teacher. Durand's work routinely sold for five times the prices of Ralph's paintings.

"Really? I didn't realize you used to teach," Susan said.

"Ralph was far and away the best instructor I ever had."

Pamela, the director of the Roadrunner, had come up behind us while we were talking to Ralph. As usual, the tiny woman wore beige. Although Pamela's fashion choices were never colorful, the same couldn't be said about her vibrant paintings, depicting exotic animals and lush scenery.

"That includes every professor I had in art school," she declared.

"Thanks, Pamela," Ralph mumbled, looking a bit uncomfortable at the effusive compliment.

"I've just been talking to Brooks, and he's organizing some kind of plein air art event with Ulysses. He promised to get the details to me tomorrow. Believe it or not, he's inviting all our members to participate.

"Brooks has certainly done an about-face," I said.

"Remember when he'd come into the Roadrunner and criticize everybody's work?"

Pamela nodded. "I think he's trying to re-invent himself as an influential figure in the art world. He couldn't succeed as an artist, but he certainly has the contacts and the money to make a name for himself as a gallery owner."

"It doesn't hurt that his wife's managing his gallery, either," I said, nodding toward the thirtyish blonde in a figure-hugging black dress and six-inch Louboutin heels, who was talking animatedly with the Suns' star. The player's wife stood by, fuming, while her husband looked at Brooks's wife with unabashed fascination.

It was the same look I'd seen on my son Dustin's face when we'd visited Brooks's former gallery in downtown Lonesome Valley one spring day when Dustin was visiting me. I hadn't seen her since that day when she'd totally ignored me and tried to high-pressure my son into buying one of her husband's awful paintings. At least, now she had some real artwork to sell.

Pamela, Ralph, Susan, Chip, and I chatted for several more minutes before we went our separate ways. I circled the gallery to look at the rest of Ulysses's paintings.

One, a mountain scene at twilight, particularly caught my attention. It looked familiar. I tried to remember where I'd seen it before. Most likely, the picture had been featured in an art magazine I'd read. I made it a point to check out every art magazine that the Lonesome Valley Library got in, just as I had when I lived in Kansas City.

"Mom, look at this!" My daughter handed me her cell phone. "Here's my selfie with Anne and Terry on Instagram."

"Great picture, Emma. The three of you look like lifelong friends. You'd never know you'd just met them a few minutes ago."

"They're super nice. Look at the rest of the pictures," she said, as she scrolled through several more shots.

Later, as we drove home, Emma kept herself busy, constantly sending text messages and replying to messages from her friends about her unexpected encounter with the famous Hollywood couple. I wondered if the meeting had been the highlight of her summer, since our day-to-day schedule had been fairly routine.

The divorce had hit both my children hard; they'd been just as shocked as I had when Ned announced he planned to divorce me. Although Emma had spent the first week of her summer vacation with her father, his new wife, and their baby, she hadn't been happy about it. Her room had been transformed into a playroom for the baby, but he wasn't old enough to use it yet, and Emma had felt that she didn't belong in the home where she'd grown up.

"Has your summer been OK, Emma?" I asked somewhat hesitantly. "You haven't even had your own bed, my house is so small."

"Sure, Mom. I like your house. It's cute and cozy. You know I'd way rather sleep on the hide-a-bed than in your room so I can stay up late and watch TV or surf the net."

"And you didn't mind working at the feed store? I know it wasn't the most glamorous job."

"It was fine. Dennis is a cool boss, and the pay wasn't bad."

Before her break started, Emma had asked me if I knew of any summer jobs in Lonesome Valley, and I'd checked with my next-door neighbor, who managed a local feed store to find out if he needed any extra help. He assured me he did, and Emma had a summer job without ever having to interview.

"Dennis said to let him know if I wanted to work at the feed store again next summer, and I told him I do."

"Emma, that's great!"

I'd hoped she'd want to spend the summer with me again next year, but we hadn't really talked about it.

As I parked in my carport, I could hear my golden retriever Laddie barking inside the house. I knew he'd heard us coming before we turned into the driveway. Somehow, he was able to distinguish the difference between my SUV and every other vehicle that came up Canyon Drive.

Laddie crowded the door as Emma and I entered, his feathery tail whipping back and forth. He wasn't satisfied until both Emma and I gave him a hug.

"I guess Mona Lisa's in one of her moods," Emma said. "Here, kitty, kitty, kitty," she called, but my persnickety calico cat didn't appear. She was probably hiding behind the sofa or under my bed, and she'd deign to grace us with her presence on her own schedule, not ours.

She finally made her appearance shortly before we went to bed for the night, sneaking into my tiny living room and pouncing on Emma's feet. Emma picked her up for a cuddle, and Mona Lisa purred loudly. My cat had pretty much forsaken me in favor of my daughter since Emma had come to stay with us for the summer. Instead of curling up in my bed at night, she snuggled with Emma.

Laddie seemed happy to have me all to himself; he didn't miss our feline companion when she deserted us for Emma.

I was afraid that Mona Lisa was going to be a very sad kitty tomorrow, after Emma left.

"Are you going to miss me when I go back to school?" Emma asked the little calico cat.

Mona Lisa emitted a loud "meow" in response, and I knew that she wouldn't be the only one who'd miss Emma when she returned to college.

Chapter 3

Two days later I was thinking how much quieter my little house seemed without my daughter's lively presence when I heard my neighbor Belle's distinctive knock on my kitchen door.

"Belle, you're back!" I exclaimed as I gave her a hug. Her little fluffy white dog Mr. Big shot into the kitchen where Laddie joyfully greeted his little buddy. They hadn't seen each other for almost three weeks while Belle and her husband Dennis had been visiting their family in Michigan.

"Do you have time to take the dogs for a walk?" she asked. "I couldn't remember whether you were scheduled to work at the gallery today."

"Sure. Laddie's raring to go. I'm working in the gallery today, but not till this afternoon. I've decided to schedule four half days a month, rather than two full days. That way, I can get some painting done on my gallery work days if I want to. To tell you the truth, I wasn't even planning on doing that today. I don't know why I have such a hard time sticking to a schedule."

"You accomplish plenty, Amanda, schedule or no schedule. I have a feeling you may be missing Emma now that she's gone back to college."

"You're right. I was just thinking about how quiet the place is without her. A walk will do me good."

I grabbed Laddie's leash and snapped it onto his collar while Belle checked Mr. Big's collar and leash to make sure they were secure. The active little dog had backed out of his collar and run off toward another dog at the park the day before Belle and Dennis left on their trip. Although we'd been able to catch up with Mr. Big, Belle didn't want to have to deal with any more of his escape-artist antics.

"All set," she said, and we were off.

"Let's take a little detour around the block before we go to the park," Belle suggested. "I want to see what's going on at that house on the other side of yours. When Dennis and I got home last night, I thought I saw a light over there. It's been vacant since the first of the year."

"We might as well go out the studio door," I said, and we all trooped through my studio to the side door, which normally I opened only on Friday evenings for studio tours. My studio had been a stop on the Lonesome Valley Artists' Studios Tour for several months. Although few lookers visited on some Fridays, I'd had enough business to make it worthwhile.

My view of the vacant house next door was obstructed by a high hedge between the two properties, so the out-of-sight, out-of-mind residence hadn't captured my attention.

"Looks like somebody's moving in," Belle commented. "All the blinds have been raised. I guess we're about to have a new neighbor."

"I hope my studio tour won't disturb them on Friday nights. Sometimes people park in front of that house."

"I think it'll be fine," Belle assured me. "It's only for three hours once a week."

We circled the next block and headed to the park. Laddie couldn't resist flopping down and rolling in the grass as soon as we arrived, and Mr. Big bounced around his pal until I coaxed my affable golden boy to continue on our way. The park was quieter than it had been a few days earlier. Like Emma, the local students had returned to school.

Somehow, I'd have to force myself to get back into my routine, too. It helped that Belle and Dennis were back from their trip. We'd become fast friends early on after my move to Lonesome Valley, and hardly a day passed that Belle and I didn't walk the dogs together or meet for coffee. We both liked to cook, and we often exchanged casseroles or desserts we'd made. Belle's husband Dennis was quite the cook in his own right, and the three of us frequently ate dinner together with Dennis presiding over his barbecue grill on their patio while Laddie and Mr. Big romped in the backyard.

After half an hour at the park, Belle reluctantly suggested that we should head for home since she had three weeks' worth of mail to sort and needed to make a run to the grocery store.

"I won't say the larder's bare," she declared, "but I definitely need some fresh veggies, fruit, and bread."

We didn't dawdle on our walk home. Mr. Big made sure he never let Laddie get ahead of him, even though it meant his taking four steps to every one of Laddie's.

"Look there," I pointed to a furniture delivery truck in front of the formerly vacant home next door. "You were right."

Two burly deliverymen exited the house and climbed into the truck, but we saw no sign of the new owner.

No matter who they were—a family or a couple, a single or roommates—I couldn't imagine that they would ever become such good friends as Belle and Dennis were to me.

Chapter 4

"I've got it!"

"Got what, Amanda?"

"Oh, sorry, Pamela," I said, as I signed in for my afternoon shift at the Roadrunner. "I guess I was thinking out loud. One of Ulysses's paintings at Brooks's gallery looked very familiar to me, but I couldn't remember where I'd seen it before. It just now came to me. One of my Mom's jigsaw puzzles—it's the exact same picture."

Pamela nodded. "Ulysses is quite the marketer, or, I should say, his wife is. She takes care of all his business arrangements, from what I understand. Ulysses's artwork has been plastered all over lots of products from t-shirts to mugs. Several companies sell the stuff, and he gets a cut of every sale."

"Sounds quite lucrative."

"I'm sure it is. He has a condo in Florida, a vacation retreat in Spain, and he lives on a ranch somewhere near Santa Fe. When I first met him, he was more of a starving artist than a tycoon. I knew him because we were both Ralph's students for a while."

The gallery door swung open, and Susan hurried in.

"I hope I'm not late," she said, a little out of breath. "There was some road construction on First Street, and traffic was at a standstill for fifteen minutes."

"You're right on the dot," Pamela said, glancing at the big clock next to the cash register.

"Oh, good. What's the scoop on the plein air event you mentioned the other evening?"

"I'm writing an email to send out to all the members. Brooks didn't give me the details until this morning. He said there'd been a slight glitch with the arrangements—something about a permit, I believe—but everything's on track now."

"The plein air paint-out will take place next Saturday morning up at Miners' Lookout from eight until noon, and the public can watch. Ulysses will be the main attraction. All the rest will be local artists, including any of our own members who want to participate.

"Then, the paintings will all be auctioned off that evening with half the proceeds going to each individual artist and half to the artist's favorite charity. What do you think? Are you both in?"

"I am," Susan said. "It sounds like fun."

"So am I," Pamela confirmed. "What about you, Amanda?"

"I don't know."

Susan painted with watercolors, and Pamela used acrylic paints. Neither would face the problems I would have since my oil paints would still be wet at the end of the morning. Besides the wet paint issue, I tended to work very slowly. I wasn't sure I could complete a painting in four hours.

"Oh, come on, Amanda," Susan urged. "We can help carry your painting so it will be safe afterwards if you're worried about wet paint."

"Well, all right. I guess I'll do it. And thanks for your offer.

That's exactly what I was worried about." I didn't want to admit the other reason for my hesitation. Neither Susan nor Pamela seemed to have any such qualms.

It wasn't unusual for me to spend forty or fifty hours on a painting. Now I'd have to finish one of my landscapes in a tenth of my usual time. I hoped I wasn't setting myself up for failure, but since I'd agreed to take part, I wasn't about to back out.

The wheels turned as I tried to decide which charity I'd designate to receive half the proceeds from the sale of my painting. Then another thought popped into my head. I certainly hoped somebody would buy it. I'd be both embarrassed and disappointed if there were no takers.

I tried to shake the negative thinking as I decided on the local pet rescue society as my charity of choice.

"Looks like we have some customers coming," Susan said, nodding toward the gallery door, where a group of women had gathered outside. A tall woman with long brown hair was speaking to the little cluster of ladies before they crowded inside.

"That's Isobel McCafferty," Pamela told us. "She came in last week to let me know she'd be giving her first tour of Lonesome Valley this week, but I thought she told me it would be tomorrow. I must have mixed up the dates."

Pamela hurried over to Isobel while Susan and I greeted the group.

"How many of you have visited Lonesome Valley before?" I asked, and about half of the women raised their hands.

"My husband and I used to come up here three or four times a year," said a white-haired woman, "so I thought our Mothers' Club might enjoy the trip, and here we are."

The club's members branched out, meandering around the gallery, while we stood by to answer any questions they might have.

"This place is every bit as nice as the galleries in Scottsdale," one woman said, as she looked at Susan's floral watercolors. "Oh, I love this one! It would go perfectly above the console in my entryway."

Hearing her comment, Susan's ears perked up, and the two were soon engaged in conversation.

Several other women gathered at the jewelry counter, so I headed there to assist them. Soon, I'd sold several pairs of earrings, a large turquoise pendant necklace, and half a dozen packets of note cards. A few minutes later, Susan successfully closed the sale of her cactus flower watercolor painting, too.

As the group left, Isobel assured Pamela that the Roadrunner would definitely remain a stop on her tours.

We'd barely recovered from the flurry of activity when Ulysses and a slender, dark-haired woman I assumed to be his wife entered the gallery. She held a phone to her ear, its case decorated with an abstract floral design, but she quickly dropped it into her purse.

"Pamela," Ulysses said, "I hardly saw you the other night." He moved in closer to her, and it looked as though he was about to hug her, but she quickly stepped back. There was an awkward split second before Ulysses introduced his wife Olivia to Pamela.

"It's nice to meet you," Pamela said politely. "I must have missed you at Brooks's gallery the other evening."

"No. Unfortunately, I wasn't able to attend. I had an important business meeting in Los Angeles that day. If my flight had been on time, I would have been there."

"That's what happens when you cut it close," Ulysses said.

Olivia glared at him. "Somebody has to take care of business!"

"Yes, yes. Of course, you're right, my dear."

An uncomfortable moment of silence followed Ulysses's attempt to mollify his wife, but Susan saved the day when she offered Olivia a tour of the gallery and led her around the divider wall, into the gallery's back area. I excused myself to return to the counter, saying I had some paperwork to catch up on, but I could still hear every word that passed between Ulysses and Pamela.

Ulysses turned to her with a weak grin on his face. "Sorry about that," he mumbled. "She gets a little over-sensitive sometimes."

Pamela shrugged.

"It's been what—twenty-five years since I've seen you. You haven't changed a bit, Pam."

"Closer to thirty, and I go by Pamela now."

"The good old days. Ralph always kept us on our toes. He's a great guy, isn't he?"

Pamela nodded. "He's one of the Roadrunner's founders. There are some of his recent paintings on the wall right behind you."

Ulysses turned around to look. "Wonderful! I hope he'll be able to come to the paint-out."

"I don't know. You saw that he was using his cane at the opening. His arthritis has really been bothering him the last week or so, and the path up to Miners' Lookout might be too much for him. But if he feels up to it, I think he'll make an effort to come."

"Well, I'm looking forward to it."

"Kind of an odd choice to hold the event at Miners' Lookout, isn't it?"

"How so?"

Pamela lowered her voice. "You know—Jill's disappearance. Surely, it can't be a pleasant memory."

Chapter 5

Windless, cool, and sunny—the weather forecast for the day of the plein air paint-out couldn't have been more perfect. I'd stowed my easel, canvas, paints, and other supplies in my SUV the day before so that all I had to do was jump in the car and take off as soon as I dropped Laddie off at Belle's.

Belle and I had scouted Miners' Lookout a few days earlier. We'd missed the turn to the winding mountain road leading to the Lookout, but now that I knew where to find it, I arrived at the gravel parking lot with time to spare. There were already several cars in the lot when I pulled in. I spotted Susan's blue Honda and parked next to her.

"Beautiful day, isn't it?" Susan said as we removed our supplies from our trunks.

"Yes, it's great. I was afraid it would be windy again today, and that would have been a disaster."

"We lucked out," Susan agreed, as several other vehicles nosed into the lot. "It looks like we check in over there." She pointed to a couple of long tables sitting next to the trailhead, the steep path that led to Miners' Lookout above.

Brooks Miller stood behind one table, distributing laminated badges to the artists who were participating in the event. I slipped the long ribbon holding my badge over my head, and Susan did the same.

Brooks had always worn a suit whenever I'd seen him. Now he looked different, but perfectly at ease, in a sweater, jeans, and sneakers. On the other hand, his wife Gabrielle, who stood behind the other table, which held bagels, bottles of water, and orange juice, definitely seemed out of her element. Although she, like Brooks, wore a sweater and jeans, her choice of footwear couldn't have been more inappropriate for the rugged terrain. Her strappy high platform sandals wouldn't have been easy to walk in anyplace, and they didn't look like they'd survive a trek up the trail, but perhaps she planned to stay at her post all morning, rather than going up to the Lookout to observe the painters.

"You're welcome to go on up to the Lookout right away, pick a spot, and set up, but no painting until eight. We'll check right before to make sure nobody starts early."

"How will we know when we can start?" Susan asked. "I don't want to jump the gun."

"The bell in this case," Brooks said, smiling. "I'll announce the start and ring a bell promptly at eight."

"Sounds good," I murmured.

We moved to the table Gabrielle stood behind and each helped ourselves to a bottle of juice. I smiled at Gabrielle, and Susan nodded. She watched us but didn't say a word.

"Real friendly, isn't she?" Susan whispered as we headed to the restroom, situated not far from the trailhead. "I suppose there's no restroom up at the Lookout."

"There isn't. Belle and I checked it out the other day."

"Figures. Good thing I'm a fast worker," she said. "Coming down here and going back up to the Lookout will cut several minutes off our four hours."

"For sure." I was still a bit worried that I wouldn't be able to complete my painting in the allotted time, so I'd selected a sixteen-inch by twenty-inch canvas to paint, although normally I preferred painting on a larger canvas.

After our pit stop, we trudged up the path to the Lookout. I was glad I'd put my paints and supplies in a backpack so that I had to carry only the easel and canvas. Even so, it was slow going, and we were happy to reach the Lookout, which offered a wonderful view of nearby mountains and the valley below. The side of the Lookout where we could see the view had a sheer drop-off, and although a couple of warning signs were posted, no fence or other barrier prevented someone who wandered too close to the edge from tumbling over.

"I'm staying well back from that," Susan said, pointing to the drop-off. "Oh, look over here. Scarlet morning glory! I can't believe it! You don't see that too often around here."

Susan set up her easel near the bright red wildflower, while she explained to me that it was fairly rare, classified as a noxious weed, and thus illegal for nurseries to sell in Arizona.

I settled on a spot nearby with a nice view of a stand of trees that I'd decided to make the focus of my painting. A few artists had already staked out their territories; others had followed us up the path and were scanning the area, deciding where they wanted to set up their easels.

I'd been surprised to learn that besides Susan, Pamela, and me, only three other Roadrunner members had agreed to participate in the event—Chip, Ralph, and Valerie, an art teacher at Lonesome Valley High School who was also a member of our gallery's board of directors. I quickly set up my easel, placed my canvas on it, and unpacked my paints and other supplies. Absorbed in my task, I didn't pay much attention as other artists set up, but when I looked around, I was startled to see that Chip had positioned himself close to the cliff's edge. He saw me staring at him and made a thumbs-up gesture, which Susan saw, too.

"I don't know what that boy's thinking," Susan said. "I'm going to try to convince him to move back."

Before she could take a step in Chip's direction, the problem resolved itself when Brooks approached Chip and insisted he move back several feet from the edge. Chip looked ruefully at Susan and me and shrugged.

"Do you know whether Ralph's still planning on coming?" I asked Susan.

"I suspect he might not make it today," she told me. "Even though he wasn't using a cane the last time I saw him, he was limping. I think the walk up the trail would be difficult at best for him."

I nodded. "Did you know Ralph held a plein air paint-out for his students in this very spot about thirty years ago?"

"No, I hadn't heard that."

"From what Pamela told me, Ulysses's first wife Jill actually left him during the paint-out. At first, everybody thought she'd wandered off and lost her way, but when they searched and couldn't find her, Ulysses reported her missing to the police. Then, he went home and found a Dear John letter from her."

"That's awful!"

"Definitely. I imagine Ulysses felt devastated at the time, but it doesn't seem to bother him anymore. He chose this spot himself for the paint-out. Pamela asked him if Miners' Lookout brought back unpleasant memories, and Ulysses told her it all happened so long ago it didn't really bother him anymore."

"Well, I guess I can understand. He's married again; he's

famous; he's rich. What's not to like? I doubt that he has a care in the world," Susan said as she looked past me and waved. "This is a first. It's Pamela, and her husband's actually with her."

"Really? I've never met him." I turned to see the tiny woman with a tall bearded man, who was carrying Pamela's easel and canvas.

"It must be nice to have a helper," Susan said when Pamela came over.

"It is," Pamela beamed. "Amanda, I don't think you've met my husband Rich. Rich, this is Amanda Trent."

Rich greeted me and Susan politely and asked Pamela where she'd like to set up her easel. Before she could answer, he looked around, saw Chip, and suggested a spot as far away from him as possible. Pamela instantly agreed, and they began unpacking her supplies.

"That's odd," Susan said. "It's the last place I would have chosen."

"Mmm," I murmured. I figured Pamela's husband disliked Chip, and I knew why, but that particular secret wasn't mine to share. I distracted Susan by calling her attention to Ulysses, who had just arrived with Olivia and a handful of admirers who stationed themselves behind him as he set up his easel and placed his canvas on it.

The last to arrive, Ulysses spoke cordially to the knot of people gathered to watch him paint while his wife set up another easel next to him.

"Surely he isn't planning on painting two pictures," Susan said, staring at the couple, but it soon became obvious that his wife was planning on doing a painting of her own.

"I knew Olivia was Ulysses's business manager, but I didn't

realize she's a painter, too," I told Susan.

"Counting Ulysses and Olivia, now we have ten artists here. Valerie's over there, near the three artists from the other galleries in town. It must be close to starting time. I guess Ralph decided not to come."

Just then, Brooks began making the rounds to verify that none of the artists had already started painting. After he'd checked, Brooks greeted everyone, reminding the visitors that they were welcome to observe but cautioning them to give the artists plenty of room to work.

"When I ring the bell, you may commence working," he said formally. "Promptly at noon, I'll ring it again, and you must stop work immediately. Now: ready, set, go!" With a flourish Brooks rang his bell, and we were off. Like a thoroughbred at the beginning of a race, I felt an urge to rush, but I'd need to pace myself in order to do a good job and finish on time.

I used burnt sienna to underpaint my canvas, establishing the composition and values of the piece.

Next to me, Susan had begun lightly sketching the scarlet morning glories that would be the focus of her watercolor painting.

Telling myself to concentrate, my quick glance at Susan was the last time I looked at anything other than my canvas or the stand of trees I was painting for the next couple of hours. I worked much more rapidly than usual, and after a while, I relaxed a bit, confident I'd finish on time.

"I'm going down to the restroom," I told Susan.

"Me, too, but you go first, and I'll keep an eye on your stuff until you get back."

I hurried down the path to the parking lot below, trying to avoid the loose pebbles that dotted the trail.

Except for Gabrielle and Olivia, the area was deserted. The two stood near the refreshments table and appeared to be engaged in an intense conversation, but as soon as they saw me, they stepped apart and stopped speaking.

I didn't linger and returned to my easel in a few minutes. As soon as I came back, Susan left. A couple of observers stepped closer to her painting to look at it, but not close enough to cause concern. Still, I kept my eye on them until they drifted off to watch Pamela. I noticed Rich continued to hover near her, occasionally casting a wary eye Chip's way. Oblivious, Chip concentrated on his painting and never looked in Pamela's direction.

"Olivia and Gabrielle seem to have hit it off. They had their heads together about something," Susan said when she returned.

We went back to our paintings, and the time flew. About eleven-thirty, Brooks made the rounds of the artists to let us know we had half an hour left. When he came our way, Susan stepped back from her easel and proclaimed, "I'm done!"

I wished I could have said the same. As it turned out, I'd just finished signing my painting when Brooks rang the bell, signaling us to stop work and step back from our easels.

He thanked the artists and spectators and invited everyone to come to the auction in the evening, which would take place in one of the meeting rooms at the resort.

I was surprised and somewhat relieved to learn that Brooks had arranged to transport all the paintings directly to the resort, and we wouldn't even have to carry our paintings down to the parking lot. A crew dressed in tan chinos and blue polo shirts sporting the Lonesome Valley Resort logo appeared, and Brooks accompanied them, giving a receipt to each artist, as the crew members carefully removed artwork to carry it away.

Ulysses talked with a small group of spectators until Brooks handed him a receipt. Then he turned around and looked at his wife's canvas.

"Let me give you Olivia's receipt," Brooks said, handing Ulysses a piece of paper.

Ulysses, who was clearly upset, frowned. "Olivia was just here a few minutes ago. Did anyone see her leave?"

Brooks sought to calm the agitated artist without much success.

"She probably went down to the parking lot," Brooks said calmly. "I wouldn't worry. She'll turn up."

"That's what they told me last time I was here, and I never saw Jill again."

Chapter 6

Brooks looked confused. Evidently, he'd never heard the story of how Ulysses's first wife had left him.

"Come on, Ulysses. I'll go down to the parking lot with you, and we'll find her," Brooks said, gathering Ulysses's supplies into his carrying case. The artist picked up his easel and accompanied Brooks. As they departed, Brooks called one of the crew members over and directed him to give the rest of the artists a receipt when they picked up their paintings.

While we waited, Pamela came over to us and whispered, "Talk about a déjà vu moment. Way too close to the last paint-out Ulysses did up here, but I'm sure this one will turn out fine. I bet Olivia probably just needed a restroom break. I doubt that there's anything to worry about. Still, it's a bit odd."

"Pamela, they're ready to take your painting," Rich called.

"Coming." She scurried off to accept her receipt from a crew member. "See you at the auction tonight," she said as she waved good-bye to us.

Susan and I were the last to leave. When we reached the bottom of the trail, we saw that the tables had been removed and most of the cars had already left the parking lot.

Brooks stood next to a white van, talking to his crew

members. Then, they shut the back doors, and two of them climbed into the front.

"Did Ulysses find Olivia?" I asked Brooks. "He seemed awfully upset."

"Oh, yes. Everything's fine. Ulysses told me she came down to their car to lie down because she had a migraine headache. I'd better get moving now, so I can meet the crew at the resort. See you later."

"You know, I think it's strange Olivia didn't tell Ulysses she was going to the car," I told Susan after Brooks left.

"So do I. No wonder the poor guy seemed so upset after what happened with Jill. Do you suppose he thought Olivia had left him, too?"

"Could be. She must know all about Jill's disappearing act, so it seems kind of mean of her not to tell him she was going to the car to lie down. Olivia must have known he'd be worried."

"Maybe she's trying to get back at him," Susan speculated. "Remember their little tiff in the Roadrunner? Olivia was plenty steamed."

"Maybe so." I stepped back, stretched, and yawned. "I'm glad the paint-out's over, anyway. I think I'll stick to studio work from now on. No four-hour deadlines."

"True enough," Susan agreed, opening her trunk and depositing her easel and supplies inside. "See you tonight. Let's hope our paintings bring some megabucks' bidding."

"Let's hope!"

Susan swung her car out of the parking lot ahead of me, and I followed her down the winding mountain road into town.

Laddie was delighted to see me when I stopped at Belle's to pick him up, but when we came into the kitchen at home, Mona Lisa didn't bother to greet us. Instead, she surveyed us from atop her kitty tree and then turned her back on us.

I seldom felt tired in the afternoon, but after I had a cheeseburger quesadilla for lunch, I found myself yawning again and decided to take a power nap. Maybe it was all that fresh air, I thought, as I drifted off to sleep with Laddie stretched out beside me and Mona Lisa, who finally decided she wanted to join us, too, curled up next to me on her favorite pillow.

When I woke, I couldn't believe that I'd actually slept for two hours. Not exactly the power nap I had planned. In a groggy state, I went to the kitchen and brewed some coffee in the hope of reviving. Luckily, it did the trick, and my thoughts turned to the upcoming auction.

I'd invited Belle and Dennis to go with me. Dennis couldn't attend because he was umpiring a softball game that evening, but Belle was keen.

"I couldn't decide what to wear tonight," Belle said when we were about to depart for the auction.

"I think what you're wearing is perfect. It's not really a formal event."

Belle looked lovely in a gauzy blue maxi dress with some gold sequin accents along the neckline and long, dangling, gold earrings that complemented her wavy salt-and-pepper hair.

I'd dressed in light layers topped by a long silk chiffon vest I'd tie-dyed in shades of green. Unfortunately, I'd discovered another gray hair among the brown as I'd put on my make-up. I'd promptly yanked it out, trying not to think about how many times I'd discovered gray hairs lately.

We had no problem finding the meeting room where the auction was to be held. Large signs directed us through the Lonesome Valley Resort to the second floor.

Outside the door, bidders were filling out their billing information before being provided with a numbered paddle that they'd hold up to bid.

I'd gone to a few antiques auctions in Kansas City, searching for a sideboard for my dining room. Those had been crowded, noisy affairs with hundreds of lots on offer and the auctioneer talking so fast I couldn't understand him. I'd tried to bid on one piece of furniture by raising my number card high in the air. When I saw the auctioneer nodding in my direction, I thought I'd won the auction, but it turned out the auctioneer had been acknowledging a bid from the man sitting behind me, instead. After that, I'd given up on auctions and purchased a sideboard from a local shop.

Belle stepped up to the table and registered as a bidder. We were both hoping she wouldn't have to do any actual bidding, but my fear that my painting might not garner any bids gave me the idea to ask her to bid if there was no interest. That way, I'd essentially be buying my own painting from myself when I paid her back.

Since I wasn't planning on bidding myself, I waited for Belle while she completed her paperwork, and we went inside to be greeted by a server offering us champagne. Definitely, not a run-of-the-mill auction. There were tables laden with hors d'oeuvres and mini desserts in the back of the room, prepared by chefs from the resort's restaurants, no doubt.

Even the seating was elegant. Instead of beaten-up folding chairs, well-padded, high-backed armchairs had been set out in neat rows for the occasion. They looked like chairs that might have been in guest rooms at the resort, although I didn't know that from personal experience. Lonesome Valley Resort boasted a five-star rating and was way out of my price range.

Our paintings were prominently displayed in the front of the room. Artists had been asked to provide a title for their works, and we'd been handed a list of the paintings for sale on our way in. They were arranged in alphabetical order by the artist's name, except for Ulysses's painting, the one that would be auctioned off last as the grand finale. Next to each listing, the name of the artist's chosen charity appeared.

"Shall we take a closer look?" I asked Belle, who readily agreed.

We joined a small group at the front. It was amazing to me that all the artists had completed their works in only four hours. A burgundy velvet rope prevented the attendees from coming too close to the paintings, a few of which, like mine, were oils and not entirely dry.

The front rows had filled up quickly, so we found seats about halfway back and waited for the auction to start. I looked around for Susan, but I didn't see her yet. Pamela and Rich sat a few rows behind Belle and me. We waved as we spotted each other. Like the opening for Ulysses's show at Brooks's new gallery that I'd attended with Emma, several celebrities showed up. I didn't recognize all of them, but Belle, who kept up on the latest in Hollywood, clued me in.

It was about ten minutes after seven, with no sign that the auction would begin soon, and people were starting to get a bit restless.

""I think I'll go get one of those little chocolate mousses from the dessert table," I said. "Would you like me to bring you one?"

"Yes, thanks. I don't know how we resisted earlier."

Belle and I loved chocolate. The only reason I'd passed up the mousse in the first place was that it would have been a little difficult to eat while we looked at the artwork.

Dainty silver spoons were laid out beside the little glasses of chocolate mousse. I took a couple napkins and dessert plates and set a serving of mousse on each, along with a little spoon. As I helped myself, I heard Brooks, who was standing by the door nearby, talking in a low voice to Gabrielle.

"Have you seen Ulysses?" Brooks asked. "He was supposed to be here half an hour ago."

"No, and he hasn't called me, either."

"I don't want to delay the auction much longer. If he doesn't show up soon, we'll have to start without him."

"I'll give him a call," Gabrielle said, pulling her cell phone out of her glitzy gold mesh evening bag. She shook her head. "No answer; I'll keep trying."

She nudged her phone and held it up to her right ear, covering her left ear with her hand. The buzz in the room had grown considerably louder as the bidders awaited the start of the auction.

Brooks frowned. "Unbelievable! I could wring his neck," he whispered, but his voice carried, and a few people in the back row turned around. Brooks smiled and put on his master-of-ceremonies happy face.

"We'll get started in just a few minutes," he assured them.

Gabrielle stepped out into the hallway and looked around.

"Here he comes now," she told Brooks.

Ulysses, looking pale and drawn, took Brooks by the arm. "I have to talk to you. It's important."

"Sure, but it'll have to wait until the end of the auction. We need to get this show on the road right now!"

Chapter 7

Brooks strode purposefully to the front, and I returned to my seat and handed Belle her dessert plate with the lovely little chocolate mousse. I finished mine in only a few bites, but it was delicious while it lasted.

Brooks announced that the auction was about to get underway. He thanked all the artists who'd participated and added that free framing would be available with each high bidder's purchase. I hadn't heard that before, but after Brooks explained he had just opened a frame shop next door to his gallery downstairs in the resort's mall, I figured he was using the perk for publicity for his latest enterprise. A murmur of approval rippled through the crowd.

"Sounds like that'll cost him a small fortune. Did you know about the free framing?" Belle asked.

"No, he never said a word. It's a great incentive, though."

Brooks started the bidding with Susan's watercolor, but first he introduced her and asked her to stand to say a few words about her designated charity, a society dedicated to providing scholarships for promising art students.

I gulped. I'd always had a fear of public speaking, but I knew I'd have to force myself to get a grip before Brooks called on me.

Susan's watercolor fetched a very respectable price with several bidders vying for the lovely painting, simply titled "Scarlet Morning Glories."

Unlike the auctioneers I'd encountered when I'd attended antiques auctions, Brooks took his time, playing the genial host, always with positive comments as he encouraged the bidders to go higher. His formula worked well, and the crowd seemed happy and engaged. When he called on me, I managed to get through my talk about the Lonesome Valley Animal Rescue Society and its good work. By the time I finished, I was actually shaking, and I sank back into my cushy chair, grateful to be done, as Brooks proceeded to call for bids on my colorful landscape. I was relieved that there were several bidders. Like the artwork that had been sold previously, mine fetched a good price, so I felt both relieved and happy. So was Belle, who'd never had to raise her number paddle, because she'd been a little nervous about bidding,

Finally, Brooks came to the last painting. Like mine, it was an oil painting. Unlike mine, which was in a style I called expressionistic abstract, Ulysses's landscape was in the same hyper-realistic style that Ralph favored. Ulysses looked almost ill as he stood and acknowledged a round of applause from the audience. He spoke briefly, almost by rote, about his favorite charity.

I wondered if perhaps Ulysses really was ill. Maybe both he and Olivia were coming down with a bug. She'd had a headache earlier and hadn't accompanied Ulysses to the auction, even though her painting was on offer, too, and Brooks had filled in to talk about her charity. He hadn't said she was sick, though, only that she was unable to attend.

Brooks quickly picked up the pace, making up for Ulysses's

lack of enthusiasm. As expected, Ulysses's artwork brought the highest price of the evening by far. I didn't need Belle to tell me who placed the top bid because I recognized the actor as the star of a popular TV drama I'd watched for years.

After the auction ended, the crowd thinned, but several people remained. Belle saw a friend of hers who'd been sitting on the other side of the room and went over to talk with her, while I couldn't resist visiting the dessert table again and snagging a pink petit four decorated with a cute design of white rosebuds and green leaves.

Brooks and Ulysses had sequestered themselves in a small alcove not far from where I was standing. I could see them out of the corner of my eye. Although they spoke in low voices, somehow the acoustics of the room amplified their conversation, and I could hear them clearly.

"How soon can I get my money?" Ulysses asked urgently.

"We're going to disburse the funds Monday."

"I tell you I need the cash now! And I need all of it! Can't you make some arrangements?"

"Calm down, Ulysses. You're being totally unreasonable. You know the banks are closed on the weekend."

"You don't understand. Olivia's been kidnapped!"

Chapter 8

"They're holding her for ransom, and I can't raise the half a million without the money from the auction. Most of my assets aren't liquid. You have to help me!"

"Olivia wasn't in your car after the paint-out, was she?"

"No! All I found in the car was a ransom note."

"We need to go to the police right away."

"I forbid it! They said they'd kill her if I told the police." Ulysses grabbed Brooks by his lapels. "Please, man, you've got to help me. And promise you won't involve the police!"

Suddenly they stopped talking and looked in my direction. Frowning, Brooks approached me. He stood uncomfortably close as he leaned over to whisper in my ear.

"I think you may have heard something you weren't intended to hear. Am I right?"

I nodded and Brooks took me by the elbow and steered me over to Ulysses.

"You heard?"

"Yes, and I think you should report it to the FBI. They can help you."

"No way. The kidnappers warned me. They said they're watching me. I can't take any chances. You must promise not to breathe a word about this to a soul. It's my decision."

Just then, Ulysses's cell phone rang. He quickly answered, and his face contorted in fear as he listened. Brooks and I could hear a tinny, robotic voice emanating from the phone. Ulysses never had an opportunity to say a word before the caller hung up.

"He's watching us right now!" he said. "He told me I was with Brooks Miller and Amanda Kaye Trent. Now do you believe me? If we call the police, he's going to kill Olivia!"

I scanned the room, but I didn't notice anyone looking our way. All the people who remained were engaged in their own conversations. They weren't paying any attention to us.

Although I thought Ulysses should call in the FBI, I could understand the reason he remained adamant. He believed the kidnapper's warning that he'd kill Olivia if he went to the authorities for help.

"I think we have to respect Ulysses's wishes, Amanda," Brooks said. "He's more interested in keeping Olivia safe than in catching the kidnappers."

"I realize that, but . . . ."

"I'm begging you," Ulysses pleaded, desperately. "Don't say a word!"

"All right," I agreed reluctantly. "I'm so sorry this happened. I hope you'll be able to raise the ransom money."

"Don't worry about that," Brooks told me. "I'll take care of it."

I left the two of them huddled together in the alcove and found Belle still chatting with her friend on the other side of the room. I felt sick with dread after what I'd heard and quite powerless to do anything about it. I thought Ulysses's decision not to inform the police was a bad one, but I also understood his refusal, especially after he'd received the creepy phone call.

Belle noticed that I was unusually quiet on the way home, but I explained by fibbing, claiming I had a splitting headache.

That night, I lay awake, thinking about what poor Olivia must be going through. Ulysses had to be out of his mind with worry, but I knew Brooks would make sure he raised every dollar of the ransom. Brooks belonged to one of the wealthiest and most influential families in Arizona. Raising cash, even on the weekend, shouldn't present a problem for him. When he'd said he'd take care of it, he'd sounded resolute.

I kept thinking about the weird phone call and its implications. The kidnapper had known Brooks's name and my name, but since I seldom used my middle name, I assumed he had attended the auction, where my name on the program was listed as Amanda Kaye Trent. When I'd stood after Brooks introduced me, the kidnapper had heard my name and seen what I looked like. I was convinced that the kidnapper, or one of them, had attended the auction. Whoever it was must have had to leave the room and find a private place to make the phone call to Ulysses so that he could use some kind of equipment to alter his voice. I kept thinking of the kidnapper as a man, but I realized a woman could be involved, and probably more than one person was participating.

How had they managed to snatch Olivia, right out from under our noses, at a public event? No doubt about it—she had vanished into plein air!

Chapter 9

Sunday, I felt anxious to learn what was happening, but, of course, Brooks and Ulysses had no reason to let me know. I'd stumbled onto the knowledge of the kidnapping by chance. Again, I wondered whether I should have promised to keep quiet about it since the FBI had the experience to deal with the situation. On the other hand, I could understand why Ulysses didn't want to involve them. The threatening phone call he'd received while we were talking had probably influenced me, too.

Slowly, the hours ticked by, as I worked on a commissioned pet portrait of two Siamese cats, striving to capture their lively natures. Their pet parents had sent me several videos of the playful pair, and I almost felt as though I knew them, even though I'd never met them in person.

I had Emma to thank for this particular commission. She'd set up a website for me, devoted just to my pet portraits. I didn't remove examples or references to this part of my art business from my artist's website, which showed the full range of my work, but I thought the separate website devoted to pet portraits was a good idea. Emma had shared images of my pet paintings extensively on social media, generating some traffic for the new site, and I'd already gained commissions for two portraits from inquiries through the website.

My income from my art business fluctuated wildly. So far, I'd been extremely lucky that whenever the balance in my checking account plunged, I'd sold a painting. I was hoping that the pet portrait side of my business could eventually provide some stability. Although budgeting wasn't exactly my strong suit, and neither was solving cash flow issues, so far I'd managed to muddle through.

Artists like Ulysses didn't have such problems, I thought, but perhaps I was wrong about that. He'd said he needed the proceeds from the sale of his auctioned painting to have enough to pay Olivia's ransom, but then again, he'd said most of his assets weren't liquid. According to Pamela, Ulysses was a very rich man, indeed.

I took an occasional break from my painting to check the local news on my laptop, although I realized that if Ulysses were successful and Olivia safely returned home, he'd probably keep the entire incident to himself. By evening, I couldn't stand the suspense any longer, so I decided to call Brooks in hopes that he'd be willing to tell me what was happening, but it proved an impossible task. I didn't know his cell phone number, and when I called the resort and asked to speak with him, my call was directed to his voice mail. I left a message before I called back and explained to the resort's switchboard operator that I'd left a message, but that I needed to get in touch with Brooks right away. She told me he "wasn't in," and she refused to give me his landline or cell phone number. I fretted, but there was nothing else I could do.

About half an hour later, Brooks called me.

"Thanks for calling me back. You must have heard my message."

"No, I didn't. Uh, Amanda, I'm calling because I have a big favor to ask you. Olivia's life depends on it."

"What is it?" I asked as my stomach did flip flops.

"The kidnappers have contacted Ulysses, but they don't want him to deliver the ransom. They want you to do it."

"Me?" I croaked.

"Yes. My guess is that they figure you already know about the kidnapping, and they don't want to have to deal with Ulysses possibly trying to pull some heroics or maybe deciding to track them down."

"But. . . ."

"Look, I know it could be dangerous. They demanded that you come alone."

I could hear Ulysses in the background, asking Brooks to hand him the phone, and the next thing I knew, Ulysses was begging me to deliver the ransom money. He assured me that all I needed to do was drop off a gym bag and leave immediately.

"What's the back-up plan if I don't do it?" I asked.

"There isn't one! Don't you understand? They know who you are, and they want to see you, nobody else."

"All right," I said against my better judgment, but I figured the kidnappers had nothing to gain from harming me. "When and where?"

"We don't know yet. They're supposed to call back in an hour to tell me."

Brooks came back on the phone and he would have offered to send one of the resort's limos to pick me up, but the kidnappers insisted that I drive my own car. That wasn't exactly welcome information because it meant they not only knew who I was, but they also knew what kind of vehicle I drove.

The light was already fading from the sky as I grabbed my bag and keys from the kitchen counter. I gave Laddie a hug and told him to be a good boy. I would have picked up Mona Lisa for a quick cuddle, but she was nowhere to be seen. On my way out, I turned on the kitchen light and the light in my carport, so I wouldn't be coming home to a dark house.

If I was coming home.

As I drove to the resort to meet Ulysses and Brooks, I felt scared, but I kept reminding myself that the kidnappers really had no reason to harm me. Still, we were dealing with criminals—people who'd abducted Olivia and threatened her life. And there was no guarantee that they would keep their promise to release her after they collected the ransom.

Brooks met me at the valet parking area of Lonesome Valley Resort and directed one of the valets on duty to keep my SUV available, rather than moving it to the reserved parking lot. Then, he led me upstairs to the suite he'd provided for Ulysses and Olivia during their stay in Lonesome Valley.

Normally, I would have taken in every detail of the huge suite, decorated in Southwestern style, but I felt too wound up to concentrate on anything other than my role in helping Olivia come home alive.

Brooks produced a gym bag with the Lonesome Valley Resort logo on it. It looked like any other bag except for a white scrape on one of its black handles. He unzipped it and showed me the cash.

"Half a million in unmarked hundreds," he said. "That's what they asked for."

"We want to follow their instruction exactly," Ulysses said. "We're not going to try to track them down. I'm sorry that they specified you have to come alone. I asked them to let me deliver the money, but they refused."

While we waited for the kidnappers to call with the location for the ransom drop, Brooks made sure that we all had each others' cell phone numbers in our phones, so we could communicate, if necessary.

"They should have called by now," Ulysses said, as he paced back and forth. "Why haven't they called?"

Brooks glanced at his Rolex. "It's been exactly fifty-eight minutes since their last call."

A few more minutes passed without a call.

"Why haven't they called?" Ulysses fretted. "It's over an hour now."

Another ten minutes went by, as Ulysses became more and more agitated, but there wasn't a thing he could do. He was completely at the mercy of the kidnappers.

Finally, the call came, twenty minutes past due.

Ulysses answered immediately and jotted down my instructions: come alone; drop the cash in a trash bin behind the tennis courts at East Park; leave immediately without looking back.

"Ready?" Brooks asked, picking up the gym bag.

I nodded, and he accompanied me to my car, which the valet had parked close to the resort's entrance. He put the gym bag on the passenger seat.

"Be careful, Amanda, and call me after you've dropped off the bag, but not until you're well away from the park. Ulysses said they're going to let him know where to pick up Olivia."

"OK."

I was so nervous I took a wrong turn on my way to the park and had to double back. When I reached the park, I saw two vehicles in the parking lot next to the tennis courts. I noted that one was a black pickup truck and the other a silver Toyota, although I doubted that either car belonged to the kidnappers.

Two feeble street lamps provided the only illumination. The lights on the tennis courts had been turned off. I knew they were controlled by an automatic timer, set to go off at nine in the evening, because Emma and I had batted some tennis balls around on these very courts a few times during her visit. Since I was no match for her, she always won every game we played. How I wished I were here to play tennis with Emma!

A sidewalk ran all the way around the four tennis courts. The bin was supposed to be behind the courts. I picked up the bag and my cell phone and followed the sidewalk around to the left. I thought perhaps I'd need the flashlight on my cell phone to see in the dark area behind the courts, but there was just enough light from the puny lamps in the parking lot that I didn't need to use my phone.

I spotted the trash barrel on the back side of the courts, but I stopped short when I heard people talking. It sounded as though they were getting closer, so I crouched behind the trash can, hoping I was out of sight. I peeked cautiously around the bin and saw two teenage girls heading toward the parking lot. They didn't even look my way, but I waited until I heard car doors closing before I stood and deposited the gym bag in the barrel.

Then I walked quickly back to my car. I thought I heard a noise behind me, but, as instructed, I didn't look back. I kept walking until I reached my car. My hands were shaking so badly that it took three tries to put my key into the ignition. Once I started my SUV, I wheeled out of the parking lot with a screech of tires as I accelerated. After I drove several blocks and saw no headlights behind me, I stopped at an all-night supermarket and called Brooks.

Chapter 10

I drove home to an enthusiastic greeting from both Laddie and Mona Lisa. They looked so adorable as they crowded close to me that I rewarded them each with a treat.

Keeping my phone close so that I could answer right away when Brooks called, I made myself some cinnamon toast and cocoa, figuring some comfort food couldn't hurt. Laddie lay next to me, his chin resting on my foot, as I sat at my little table and munched on my toast while Mona Lisa perched on the chair opposite me, eyeing my snack, even though she would have turned her nose up at it had I offered her a piece.

She graced me with her mysterious Mona Lisa smile, and I wondered what she was thinking, but, of course, it would forever remain a mystery.

My ringing phone interrupted my reverie, and I snatched it up and quickly scrolled to answer Brooks's call.

"I have good news and bad news," he announced, although, thankfully, he didn't keep me in suspense. "Olivia is fine—not so much as a scratch on her—but Ulysses is in the hospital."

"Oh, no! What happened?"

"I picked up Olivia myself at the truck stop. When Ulysses didn't show up, she called the resort. Of course, the kidnappers had disposed of her cell phone, so she had to convince the store clerk that it was an emergency before he'd let her use their business phone. She was practically hysterical by the time I arrived. Once I made sure she was all right, we drove around, looking for Ulysses, but we couldn't find him, so I took Olivia back to their suite at the resort. That's when the police showed up, looking for a relative of Ulysses. Luckily, he was driving one of the resort's cars, and the night clerk recognized his name."

"What happened?"

"An accident. Evidently, it was a hit and run. The back of his car was smashed in, and he ended up in a ditch on the outskirts of town. He must have gotten lost on the way to pick up Olivia, because the accident happened out on the highway. Anyway, we're at the hospital now, and we've just spoken to his doctor, who told us he should be fine. He has a concussion, and he's suffered some bumps and bruises, so they're keeping him overnight for observation. We'll pick him up tomorrow afternoon as soon as the doctor releases him."

"Poor Ulysses! After everything he's been through with the kidnapping, then this has to happen. I'm glad they're both all right."

"I want to thank you again for your help, Amanda. You really went above and beyond for someone you barely know. Both Olivia and Ulysses are very grateful. In fact, Ulysses wondered if you wouldn't mind stopping by the hospital in the morning so that he can thank you in person."

"Oh, well, uh, sure. I guess I could do that if that's what he wants."

"Great! Well, I'd better take Olivia back to the resort now so that she can wind down and Ulysses can get some sleep. It's been a stressful day for everybody."

"That's for sure." I still couldn't quite believe that I'd delivered a half-million-dollar ransom to a kidnapper, but I was very relieved that Olivia had been released unharmed. It was bad luck that Ulysses had been involved in a traffic accident, but since his doctor had told Olivia and Brooks that he'd be OK, I could go to sleep without worrying about either the artist or his wife. Even so, it took me several hours to relax enough so that I felt I'd be able to sleep, but when I finally did go to bed, I made up for my lack of sleep the previous night.

The next morning, I walked Laddie to the park before we had breakfast. I would have asked Belle to come along with Mr. Big, but it was a bit too early for her. She was something of a night owl, often staying up late, and she preferred to sleep in whenever she could. I was bursting to tell her about the kidnapping, now that Olivia was back safe and sound, especially since I knew I could count on her discretion not to tell anybody except Dennis, of course.

After I fed Laddie and Mona Lisa, I decided to make some date muffins for my own breakfast. I'd bought the dates at a farmers' market in Prescott, directly from the farmer who'd grown them. He'd driven up to Northern Arizona from the Yuma area to sell his sweet Medjool dates at the market. I smiled as I chopped the dates, remembering what fun Belle and I had had shopping at the outdoor market and discovering all kinds of goodies.

I popped the muffins into the oven and brewed some strong tea while I waited for the muffins to bake. They were a perfect golden brown when I removed them from the oven and tested them with a toothpick. I lingered over my tea, enjoying a warm muffin so much I couldn't resist having a second.

I hated to go to the hospital to see a patient empty-handed, and I thought maybe Ulysses would enjoy some homemade muffins after a breakfast of hospital food, so I arranged a few in red plastic wrap, set them in a small wicker basket, and added a red ribbon, tying it with a simple bow. Satisfied with my handiwork, I changed from my dog-walking jeans and sneakers into tan linen pants, a turquoise blue top, and sandals. I draped one of my tie-dyed silk scarves around my shoulders and arranged the folds. Its turquoise and cinnamon hues went perfectly with my top. I fiddled with the knot until I was satisfied with the way it looked, and I was soon ready to go.

Laddie nuzzled me and whimpered softly when he realized that I was about to leave the house without him. He frequently visited Belle to hang out with Mr. Big when I was going to be gone for a while, and I knew he preferred a play date with his buddy to staying home with only Mona Lisa, who usually ignored him, for company. Gazing into his big brown eyes as I petted him, I assured him I'd be back soon. I felt slightly guilty for leaving him, even though I knew he'd be perfectly fine.

I hadn't had occasion to visit Lonesome Valley Hospital since I'd moved to town. When I arrived there, I found the small parking lot in front packed. I drove around back, looking for a place to park, but the entire area was blocked off for construction work. It appeared the hospital management planned to solve the parking problem with a new multi-story garage. I ended up parking on the street a couple of blocks away.

At the reception desk, I asked for Ulysses's room, and I was directed to the nursing station on the second floor. When I stepped off the elevator I was shocked to find the nursing station for the hospital's intensive care unit right in front of me. There was a small waiting area to the right, which I didn't notice until I heard someone calling my name. I turned to see Brooks rising from one of the chairs.

"It's bad news, I'm afraid. Ulysses is in a coma!"

Chapter 11

"But I thought the doctor said he was going to be fine."

"The doctor was wrong," Brooks said grimly. "They've called in a specialist."

"I'm sorry. I'm just stunned. I brought him some homemade muffins," I said lamely, holding up the red, plastic-wrapped basket.

"I'll see that Olivia gets them. I'm sure she'll appreciate the gesture." Brooks reached for the little basket, and after I handed it over, he set it on the end table, where he'd put his laptop when I arrived.

"Olivia must be worried sick."

"She is. I insisted that she go down to the cafeteria to get a cup of coffee. Unfortunately, there's not much I can do for her here, other than keep her company, but I need to get back to the resort. I'm just waiting for Gabrielle to take my place. She'll stay with Olivia for a while, at least."

I nodded. There was nothing I could do, either. I returned to the elevator, pressed the down arrow, and waited. In less than a minute, the elevator door slid open, but since the going-up indicator was lighted, I decided to wait until it came back down before boarding.

Gabrielle, dressed in a navy sheath and red-soled Louboutins, emerged from the elevator. Giving her long blond hair a flip, she walked past me, without acknowledging my presence, and gave Brooks a quick kiss on the cheek.

"What's that?" she asked, pointing to the basket of muffins that sat next to Brooks's laptop.

"Amanda brought some homemade muffins for Ulysses. I said I'd give them to Olivia."

"You'll do nothing of the kind," she said, picking up the basket and depositing it in the trash can.

Gabrielle had her back to me, but Brooks glanced my way, a look of embarrassment on his face.

About that time, the elevator arrived, its door opening with a little dinging tone. Saved by the bell, I hopped inside and stepped to the back, past a couple of nurses, out of Brooks's sight. He wasn't the only one who felt embarrassed, but my own embarrassment was quickly turning to anger, although I admit I felt a bit hurt, too.

I wondered what had possessed Gabrielle to discard the basket. If she had something against me, I had no idea what it could be. I'd encountered her only a few times in my life before today. The first time I ever saw her was in Brooks's former art gallery in downtown Lonesome Valley, but that had been several months ago in the spring, when Dustin had visited me, and I was showing him around Lonesome Valley for the first time. Although she'd paid plenty of attention to my son, she'd never spoken to me. I hadn't seen her again until Emma and I attended Ulysses's opening at Brooks's new gallery in the resort's mall, but that was from across the room, and we never really crossed paths. She'd been at the paint-out and the art auction, and we hadn't spoken either time. In fact, I was pretty much the invisible woman, as far as she was concerned.

Except for one time.

I remembered the one occasion when she'd actually noticed me, now that I thought about it. She and Olivia had been talking when I descended the path at the paint-out to use the restroom, and as soon as they noticed me, they'd stopped talking. I'd felt like an intruder, even though I'd had as much right be be there as they had.

When the elevator reached the first floor, the nurses filed out, and I followed, almost forgetting that I had another errand to attend to before I left the hospital.

Across from the reception desk was the hospital's gift shop, run by a group of volunteers called Friends of Lonesome Valley Hospital. I'd researched the gift shop and added it to my short list of the retailers Belle had suggested I pitch to carry my silk scarves in their shops. I reached into my bag and pulled out a business card, my wholesale price list, and a full-color brochure I'd had printed at a local copy shop. Taking a deep breath, I entered the gift shop. I'd been hesitant to make personal sales calls and had mailed my information to a few local shops, instead, but I realized that I'd have to follow up with personal calls if I hoped to make any sales.

Inside, two women wearing blue cover-all aprons with the hospital's logo embroidered on the patch pockets greeted me politely and asked how they could help me.

I explained my mission, taking off my yard-square scarf and holding it up so that they could see my design more easily.

"That's really beautiful," the younger woman said.

"Yes. I love the colors," her white-haired companion agreed. "We can pass your information on to Xena. She's our treasurer, and she does all the ordering. She's not here today, but if you'd like to speak to her, she's scheduled to work tomorrow morning. Maybe you could drop back then."

"All right. I can probably do that." I thanked them and draped my scarf back over my shoulders, fastening it with a fancy knot.

I should have remembered to find out who the decision maker was before showing up for a cold call, but now that I knew she'd be in the shop the next day, I'd try again.

As I left the gift shop, I heard someone calling my name. I looked around and spotted Olivia, a large Styrofoam cup in her hand, coming toward me.

"Amanda, I want to thank you for what you did for me," she said. "I know Ulysses wanted to thank you, too, but unfortunately. . . ."

"Brooks told me. I'm so sorry."

"I just can't believe it. Last night the doctor said he was going to be fine. I never should have left him here alone."

"He had a whole staff to look after him, and even the doctor didn't suspect he'd take a turn for the worse. Besides, you'd had quite an ordeal yourself."

"Yes, well, I'd better get back upstairs."

I thought it understandable that she didn't want to talk about it.

She scurried off, giving me a quick wave as she headed for the elevator.

On the way home, I stopped at the supermarket to pick up some salmon and baby carrots. My golden boy had succeeded in making me feel a wee bit sorry for leaving him home this morning, rather than taking him to Belle's, and even though Mona Lisa didn't seem to care whether I left her or not, I planned to share some tidbits of my salmon lunch with both her and Laddie.

Mona Lisa must have smelled the salmon before I reached the kitchen door; she pounced on my feet the minute I opened it. Laddie wasn't far behind as he ran to me, elated with joy, his tail whipping back and forth. Although I suspected Mona Lisa's enthusiasm had more to do with the fish than it did with me, it was still nice to be wanted, I thought, as I set the plastic grocery bag on the counter and stooped to pet my furry companions.

After lunch, I played with Mona Lisa, flipping her favorite feather toy back and forth while she chased it. Laddie lay beside me, watching the game, but, wisely, not trying to participate. He knew his turn was coming. After I returned the feather to Mona Lisa's toy basket, she leaped to the top of her kitty tree and settled herself with her chin resting on her paws. Laddie and I went out to the backyard for a game of fetch. By the time we finished, he was panting, and I was dripping with perspiration. A cool morning had turned into a warm afternoon, and we moved into the shade on the patio. I relaxed in my chaise lounge while Laddie stretched out beside me. Fatigue was catching up with me. I told myself I'd close my eyes for a minute and promptly fell asleep. An hour later, I awoke to a persistent paw patting my arm. I stretched and shook my head, still feeling somewhat groggy after we went back inside. I refreshed the water in Laddie's bowl, and he lapped it up eagerly.

By this time, I figured I wouldn't be accomplishing any creative work today. I procrastinated for a while before deciding to tackle the mid-month bills that would be coming due in the next few days. I returned my laptop from the studio, set it on my tiny dining table, and logged into my bank account. By the time I finished paying bills, the balance in my checking account was practically nonexistent. Brooks had told Ulysses that the artists' checks for their sales at the auction would go out Monday. If that were still the case, he'd mail the checks today, and they should arrive tomorrow. I planned on making a run to the bank to deposit mine and withdraw some cash since I didn't have any folding money left in my purse after spending the last of my cash at the grocery store earlier. I was making a concerted effort not to run a balance on my credit cards, but it wasn't always easy. Thanks to the sale of my painting at the auction, I'd squeak by once more this month. Next month, I could count on the last half of the payment due me when I completed my two commissioned pet portraits. Although it was hardly enough money to see me through the month, at least it was a head start.

I sighed, contemplating my on-the-edge finances, but I didn't regret moving to Lonesome Valley or my efforts to make my living from selling my artwork.

After spending the rest of the afternoon doing laundry and a few household chores, I made a salad for an early dinner and filled my pets' bowls, setting them at opposite corners of my dinky kitchen. There was barely enough room to separate them in my small kitchen. I was picking up my dishes when Laddie, his tail wagging furiously, ran to the kitchen door. This maneuver usually signaled a visit from Belle. Most guests came to my front door, and only Belle and Dennis habitually entered by the side door closest to their own house.

Before Belle had a chance to knock, I opened the door, and Mr. Big rushed in ahead of her. I shooed the dogs into the living room, out of Belle's way.

"A dozen date cookies for you," she said, as she set a plastic container on the kitchen counter.

"Sounds good, and I saved some date muffins for you and Dennis," I told her, putting a small tin next to the container she'd placed on the counter. We both laughed.

"Great minds think alike, I guess," she said. "Somehow, it never crosses my mind to buy dates at the supermarket, but I always make a point to buy them whenever I go to the farmers market.

"How about some iced tea? We can take it out on the patio."

"Yes. Let's."

Laddie and Mr. Big eagerly followed us outside, where they were free to romp around the backyard, which was enclosed by a wall. I'd found the walled backyards typical of my new neighborhood when I'd moved to Lonesome Valley. They kept cooperative dogs in, but, from what I'd been told, walls weren't always enough to keep coyotes out, so Belle never let Mr. Big go outside alone. She'd explained that coyotes have been known to attack even large dogs, so I kept a watchful eye on Laddie when he was outside, too. Mona Lisa never left the house, so I didn't have to worry about her ever encountering a coyote.

We sipped our iced tea as we sat on the patio and watched Laddie and Mr. Big playfully running around the backyard. Belle was astonished when I told her the story of Olivia's kidnapping.

"It's unbelievable!" she exclaimed. "So that's why you were so quiet on the way home from the auction."

I nodded. "I wanted to tell you, but I literally promised not to tell a soul."

"Is Olivia going to report it to the police, now that she's back?"

"That's a good question. She didn't mention it when I saw

her this morning, but, of course, she was so upset about Ulysses's condition, she probably couldn't think about anything else. It's ironic, isn't it? We were so worried about Olivia, but now Ulysses is the one in danger."

"You could have been in danger yourself, Amanda. How did you ever work up the courage to deliver that ransom? I would have been petrified myself!"

"Believe me, I was shaking every second. I've never been so scared in my life."

"Thank goodness, it's over now."

"Yes, but not for poor Ulysses."

"Terrible luck. I suppose the driver who hit his car was drunk or maybe distracted by talking on a cell phone. I don't know what else would explain a driver hitting the car ahead."

"Hmm. I can think of one reason. What if it wasn't an accident?"

Chapter 12

"You think it was deliberate?"

"I don't know, but it could have been. Why didn't the other driver stop?"

"Could be lots of reasons. People don't always think clearly, especially if they've been drinking. Or the person could have been talking on a cell phone and become distracted. Maybe whoever it was didn't notice Ulysses's car until it was too late. Or maybe the driver at fault doesn't have auto insurance or has been in one accident too many. However it happened, I bet the driver knew he'd be in trouble and didn't want to face the consequences."

"You're right. I know hit-and run accidents happen all too often."

Still, I couldn't help wondering if perhaps there were a more sinister explanation. What if Ulysses had been deliberately targeted? Maybe Olivia's kidnapping had been a ruse to draw Ulysses out alone. That really didn't make any sense, though, I realized. If that was the goal, the kidnappers would have insisted that Ulysses deliver the money alone, putting him in a vulnerable position, but, instead, they'd designated me to deliver the ransom. Belle was probably right, and we could put

Ulysses's accident down to bad luck.

I told Belle about the second sales call I planned to make to the hospital gift shop, and she encouraged me, offering to come along with me, wearing the vibrant green silk scarf I'd made her for her birthday.

"Every time I wear it, I get compliments. What do you think?" she asked.

"Sure, and I'll wear a different one from yesterday. Maybe we can wow Xena."

"Xena? Not Xena Mareno?"

"I don't know. The ladies never mentioned her last name. Xena's not a very common name, though."

"No, it isn't. If she's who I think she is, Xena's not her given name, anyway. She adopted it because she likes it better than Sunflower."

"Her parents actually named her Sunflower?"

"So she told me, and she hates it, although I guess they always called her Sunny when she was a kid."

"That's not so bad."

"Unfortunately, some of her classmates delighted in spelling her nickname S-o-n-n-y, so when the family moved here, she told everybody her name was Xena. I met her at the library. We usually both sign up to volunteer on Wednesday afternoons, so I often see her there. Oh, I hope it turns out to be the same Xena. I just know she'll order your scarves."

"That would be great, if she did, and it would make the hospital gift shop my first wholesale account. Every little bit helps."

"If you get one account, you can get more, kind of like a snowball effect."

"But what if they want an exclusive deal? They might not

like it if other gift shops or boutiques are selling the same items."

"That's just it. They won't be the same items. Every scarf you make is unique, and lots of women like the idea that they have a one-of-a-kind accessory. They know they'll never see anyone else wearing exactly the same scarf."

"That's true enough."

My ideas about how to pursue my art business had expanded since I'd first moved to Lonesome Valley. At the time, I'd been focused on becoming a member of the Roadrunner Gallery and adding my art studio as a stop on the Friday night studio tours that the local Chamber of Commerce promoted. I'd soon learned that, while both of those endeavors formed a solid basis for my art business, they alone weren't enough to sustain it. Thus, my expansion into pet portraits and silk scarves, which I tie-dyed or painted with dye in abstract designs. I'd had lots of encouragement from Susan and Pamela, both longtime members of the Roadrunner.

Emma, Dustin, Belle, and Dennis had all helped me, too. Emma had come up with the idea of setting up a separate website to promote commissioned pet portraits. Dustin had personally driven a commissioned landscape back to Kansas City, a twelve-hundred-mile trip, and helped the buyers hang it in their den. Belle had encouraged me to pitch my scarves to local boutiques and gift shops. Dennis had made my portable sign for the Friday night studio tour and installed lights along the sidewalk that led to my studio. Thinking about all the people who'd helped me along the way, I teared up. Of course, Belle noticed right away.

"What's wrong, Amanda?"

"I'd never have made it this far without help. I'm not much

of a businessperson," I sniffed, pulling a tissue from my pocket.

"You're doing just fine. You should be proud of all you've accomplished. And don't sell yourself short, either. You're the one who's making it all work."

"With a lot of help from my friends."

"Who are happy to lend a hand," Belle said, finishing my sentence. "Most of the time you're the one doing all the heavy lifting."

"Thanks, Belle." I had occasional moments when my self-confidence waned, but Belle always encouraged me to persevere.

"You know what? Thinking about how each of your scarves has a unique design made me realize that we should come up with a hang tag for the scarves."

"Well, I have those little tags with the care instructions that I sew to the hems."

"Right, I know you need those, but I was thinking of a small piece of card stock that could emphasize each scarf as a one-of-a-kind piece of wearable art. Also, we can thread the scarf through the center and then hang it on a display."

The look of confusion on my face inspired her to offer to make up a sample.

"Wait right here," she said. "I'll be back in a minute."

Seeing Belle heading for the back door, Mr. Big ran to her.

"Stay here with Laddie and Amanda," she told him. "Mommy will be right back." The little dog seemed to understand. He went back to Laddie who was snoozing and curled up beside him.

When Belle returned, she suggested we sit at the picnic table, where she laid out ivory card stock, scissors, paper, and a small case which she opened to reveal a calligraphy set. She fitted a nib and an ink cartridge onto the pen before drawing a mock-up of a tag on the card stock. It had a round hole in the center and a curved open top edge similar to tags used for displaying men's ties. She carefully inked the label and passed it to me to inspect.

"This looks great." She'd written "Just for You," "Hand Dyed," and "One-of-a-Kind" around the circular hole in the center, and on the back, "Wearable Art from the Amanda Trent Studio."

"You could offer each wholesale account a counter display rack for your scarves." Belle quickly sketched a diagram. "See, a dowel rod here and a cardboard display head here, something like they use to display necklaces, only you would have a scarf draped around it. I know Dennis could whip a couple up in no time, and we'll take one with us tomorrow. I'll make a dozen tags tonight, so we can take twelve scarves and demo the display." Belle's eyes twinkled with enthusiasm.

"That sounds wonderful. I hope Dennis won't mind."

"You know he won't. Just keep the pies coming. That's all the thanks he wants."

"No problem. In fact, I'll whip up his favorite pecan pie and bring it over later this evening. I'd better check my stock of scarves, too, just to make sure I have enough."

"Don't forget to update your wholesale price list with the information about providing a free display rack with an initial purchase of twelve scarves."

"They have to buy a dozen to get the rack free?"

"Right. Otherwise, they can buy it if they want to."

"How much should I say it costs, in that case?"

"You want them to know they're getting something valuable, so let's say they can buy one for a hundred and fifty dollars."

"Wow! OK. Will do. Looks like I have a new sales manager."

Chapter 13

Dennis was working on the display stand later that evening when I delivered the pecan pie, and Belle was lettering the card stock labels by hand with her calligraphy pen.

"I decided to make the head and neck silhouette from wood," he said. "It'll be sturdier than cardboard, and I can cut it out with my jigsaw. I'll sand it so it's nice and smooth. We don't want any of your customers getting a splinter."

My friends had thought of everything, and I really hoped I'd make a sale after all the effort they'd put in to help me.

The next morning, Belle and I departed in plenty of time to arrive at the hospital gift shop shortly after it opened at nine. We'd stowed the counter display stand in my large hot pink suitcase so we could roll it inside. Although the stand wasn't very heavy, it was too bulky to carry easily, especially considering that we were unlikely to snag a parking spot in the hospital's small lot. Sure enough, when we reached the hospital, we found the lot completely full, so I parked on the street, as I had the day before; only this time I found a space a little closer to the hospital.

"Belle!" an auburn-haired fortyish woman exclaimed as soon as we walked in the door of the gift shop. I figured she had to be Xena. She gave Belle a quick hug. "Are you visiting someone in the hospital today?"

"No, actually we came to see you." Belle introduced me and explained our mission, and Xena invited me to set up my display on a glass counter that contained some of the jewelry the gift shop offered for sale. Xena and Belle chatted while I arranged my scarves.

"How lovely!" she said as she gently touched the hem of a fiery reddish orange scarf. I explained that, if she bought a dozen scarves, the display stand would be free.

"I'm sure these will sell," she said. "We'll take a dozen. I'll write you a check now if you can leave this display stand here today."

"Of course. It's all yours." Belle and I high-fived with glee when Xena went into the backroom office to write the check.

"My first wholesale account," I said, "and I owe it all to you. Thanks, Belle. The tags and the display stand made all the difference."

"Well, it probably didn't hurt that I already know Xena, but I'm sure she would have made a purchase anyway."

Xena came back, a check in hand. Thanking her for her order, I tucked it into my bag.

"Minimum of three scarves to re-order, right?" she asked.

"Yes, that's right, and since you're here in town, there won't be any shipping charges. I can always swing by to drop off your order."

"Good. I'm sure I'll be seeing you again soon."

We bade Xena good-bye, and Belle told her she'd see her the next day at the library. We walked out, into the hospital's reception area, and Belle suggested we stop off in one of the little restaurants downtown for brunch. I readily agreed since

I'd been too nervous about the sales call when I woke up to eat breakfast, although I'd had some strong black tea.

"Before we leave, I should go up to the second floor to find out how Ulysses is doing."

"I'll come with you."

My large bright pink suitcase drew a few stares from some of the hospital staff as I rolled it into the elevator, but I didn't think it was that unusual. I could have been there to bring some clothes to a patient, for all they knew.

The ICU waiting room on the second floor was deserted when we arrived. A nurse sat behind a computer at the nursing station. I approached her and asked her how Ulysses was doing.

"Are you a relative?"

"No, a friend," I said. That was stretching it a bit since I barely knew the famous artist.

"I'm sorry. I can't give you a report, but you could check with his wife. She went downstairs to get a drink. I'm sure she'll be back in a few minutes."

"Maybe we can catch Olivia in the cafeteria," I said to Belle, as the nurse turned her attention back to her paperwork.

We hopped back on the elevator to return to the first floor. Several hallways led away from the main reception area. The place seemed like a maze to me, but Belle had been there before, and she knew just where to find the cafeteria.

I saw Olivia sitting alone at a table near the window. She stood and discarded her cup in a large trash receptacle. She seemed startled and not particularly happy to see me when she looked up.

"Why are you here?" she asked bluntly.

"I had some business to take care of, so I thought I'd see how Ulysses is doing as long as I was already here. This is my friend Belle. Belle, Olivia Durand,"

Taken aback by my calm response, Olivia shifted gears and greeted Belle with a polite "hello."

Turning to me, she told me that there had been no change in her husband's condition. He was still in a coma.

After I said I was sorry to hear it, I hesitated before venturing to ask her another question, but I decided to plunge ahead, anyway.

"Olivia, have you reported your kidnapping to the police yet?"

"Why would I do that? It's over, and I'm fine."

"Yes, but whoever's responsible is still at large. They may try it again with someone else."

Olivia shrugged. "I can't think about that right now. If you'll excuse me . . . ."

"Of course."

"She really didn't want to talk to you," Belle observed. "I suppose she's so concerned about her husband that she doesn't want to deal with anything else."

"Could be. Shall we splurge and have brunch at Eva's in the resort, instead of going someplace downtown? I'm buying," I said, thinking of the nice check Xena had given me.

"You're on," Belle agreed. "I hear their crepes are to die for."

"Yum. I can't wait. I'm starving. I was too nervous to eat anything this morning."

Seated at a table next to a large window overlooking the resort's golf course, we treated ourselves to the chef's wonderful crepes while our server hovered inconspicuously in the background, but never failed to appear whenever we needed something.

My eyes widened when the bill arrived, but I reminded

myself that the brunch was meant to be a splurge, and it had been so pleasant that it was well worth every cent.

"Shall we stop by Brooks's new frame shop?" I asked. "I'm kind of curious to see it."

"Sure, why not? And if you don't mind, let's stop by that little candy store here, too. They have the best chocolates."

I'd never say "no" to chocolate, as Belle well knew. As soon as our server returned with my receipt, I tacked on a generous tip. Then I put my credit card back into my wallet, and we were off to the frame shop.

Inside, there was an L-shaped counter that extended the length of the shop. Both frame samples and framed artworks were displayed on the walls behind the counter. An arched doorway opposite the counter led directly into Brooks's art gallery, so that customers didn't have to return to the mall to go next door.

"That's curious. I didn't notice that door when Emma and I attended the reception for Ulysses's show," I said, peeking into the gallery.

"That's because it wasn't there then."

I whirled around and saw Brooks coming out of the frame shop's back room with a young man who was wearing the resort's signature logo polo shirt.

"Oh, hi, Brooks. My friend and I just enjoyed a lovely brunch here at Eva's." I introduced the two as the young man ducked back into the rear work area.

Brooks looked pleased at the compliment. "Glad to hear it."

"I was curious to see the frame shop. Have all the auction buyers taken advantage of your framing offer?"

"All but one. She's having some work done to her home in Beverly Hills, so her decorator's going to take care of coordinating the frame with her new decor. Actually, she's the lady who bought your painting, Amanda. I'm a little surprised she didn't talk to you after the auction."

"I never saw her." Of course, I'd been so busy helping myself to another dessert and eavesdropping that I might not have noticed if anyone had been headed my way.

"I thought I saw a man make the high bid," Belle interjected.

"You did, but he was bidding on his mother's behalf," Brooks told us.

"Oh, I can certainly understand that," I said. "I've never had any luck bidding at auctions myself. Everything always moves so fast. I'd have somebody do it for me, if I could."

Of course, that's exactly what I'd planned for Belle to do if my painting drew no bids. She rolled her eyes, but, fortunately, Brooks didn't notice.

"By the way, we ran into Olivia at the hospital this morning, and she told us Ulysses's condition hasn't improved."

"You were at the hospital today?" Brooks frowned.

Belle jumped in. "The gift shop is one of Amanda's wholesale accounts," she proudly informed him.

Brooks's expression turned from disapproval to confusion. "You're selling art at the hospital gift shop? What—like printed note cards or something?"

"Wearable art. Dyed scarves like these we're wearing."

"Oh, I see," he said dismissively.

I ignored his attitude and plunged into deeper waters.

"Olivia also told us that she hasn't reported the kidnapping to the police. Who's to say the kidnappers won't try it again? They made half a million dollars this time. Someone could get hurt or worse next time."

Brooks's frown returned. "You promised not to tell anyone

about it," he said, eyeing Belle.

"That was before Olivia came back safe and sound."

"Who else have you told?"

"Nobody. But I really think the police should be informed so that they can investigate."

"I don't know if that's a good idea, Amanda. If word gets out that the police are involved, the kidnappers might try to retaliate against Olivia or even you."

"So it's better that they're still running around loose and the police aren't even looking for them because they know nothing about it?"

"I didn't say that. Maybe you're right, but Olivia has a lot on her plate right now, what with Ulysses's condition. I hate to add another burden."

"Brooks, could I see you for a minute?" Gabrielle stood under the arch between the two shops, her icy tone unmistakable.

"Excuse me, ladies," he said as he joined his wife.

"Looks like we're dismissed," Belle whispered.

I nodded. "We might as well go get those chocolates now. I could certainly use one."

"Chocolate makes everything better," Belle agreed, as we left the frame shop.

Brooks's ambivalence about reporting the kidnapping to the police had me stumped. I knew he'd put up some of his own money to help Ulysses raise the ransom. Brooks was a very wealthy man, and perhaps recovering the money wasn't a major concern to him, but I thought justice should be. I was very much afraid that the kidnappers, having succeeded once, would repeat their crime. Besides, it made me angry that they'd gotten away with it.

If Olivia and Brooks didn't want to report the kidnapping

to the police, maybe I should do it. I had a feeling neither would thank me for doing so, and Olivia might well be too upset to handle a police interrogation right now.

Then another thought occurred to me. A police investigation into the hit-and-run accident that had put Ulysses in the hospital was already in progress. I wondered if the police had any leads.

There was one way to find out, and I knew just who to ask.

Chapter 14

I'd have to wait a few hours before satisfying my curiosity, though.

After Belle and I picked out our chocolates, we headed for home. We'd been gone longer than we planned. Laddie would be waiting for me, and Mr. Big, home alone at Belle's, would be getting anxious, too. We'd learned not to leave the two dogs together without one of us to supervise. We'd tried it once and returned to find feathers from one of Belle's pillows all over her house. The guilty parties hadn't tried to hide the evidence. When we'd walked in the door, remnants of feathers had clung to Laddie's fur, and Mr. Big had been chewing on the piping of the pillow they'd shredded.

We were both aghast at our canines' behavior because neither dog would have pulled such a stunt if Belle or I were with them. When I'd scolded Laddie, he'd stretched out on the floor and put his paws over his eyes. He'd looked so cute, I didn't have the heart to feel angry with my normally well-behaved pet. Mr. Big had been oblivious to Belle's pronouncement that he'd been a bad dog, and he'd run circles around Belle until she picked him up to calm him. That was the one and only time we'd allowed the two culprits to stay home alone together.

Since we'd had to come back home, anyway, I decided to wait for the afternoon mail, which I hoped would contain my check from the auction, before heading out again. If so, I could accomplish two errands with one trip.

While I waited for my mail delivery, which typically came late in the afternoon, I worked on a large landscape that I planned on displaying at the Roadrunner eventually. For now, it would remain on my easel while I built it up with oil paint, layer by layer.

Luckily, my check arrived, just as I'd hoped. I quickly filled in a deposit slip and paper-clipped the checks from the auction and the hospital gift shop to it. Laddie was not a happy camper when I left him home for the second time that day, but I wouldn't be gone long this time, and since I planned to take him on an evening walk later, he didn't succeed in guilt-tripping me.

There was no line when I arrived at the bank's drive-thru window where I deposited the two checks and withdrew enough cash to buy groceries and gas for the week.

Then, I headed to the police station, hoping to catch Mike, a young patrol officer I'd first met when he'd stopped me for speeding on Main Street not long after I'd moved to Lonesome Valley, but long enough that I should have already replaced my Missouri driver's license with a new one from Arizona. I'd been grateful that he'd let me off with a warning, and he'd always been polite and helpful on other occasions, too.

What I wanted to avoid, though, was seeing Lieutenant Belmont, a gruff police detective who'd once arrested Susan for murder, even though she was innocent of the crime. He'd badgered me, too, and I didn't relish the thought of possibly bumping into him at the station. With luck, Sergeant

Martinez, whose wife was a member of the Roadrunner, would be at the front desk and could let me know where to find Mike, in which case I'd never have to cross paths with Lieutenant Belmont.

As it happened, I avoided entering the station altogether because Mike, dressed in civilian clothes rather than his uniform, was coming down the steps at the station as I parked in front. I put the passenger-side window down and called to him.

"Hi, Mike. Do you have a minute?"

"Oh, hey, Amanda. Sure, what's up?"

I got out of my SUV. The sidewalk in front of the police station, awash with blazing sunlight, didn't seem like the best place to have a conversation.

"Do you mind if we go around the corner so we can sit in the shade?"

"OK," he agreed, and we began walking toward Main Street. "It's a hot one today, all right. Good thing I'm used to it, though. I'll be moving back to Phoenix next month."

Mike had had his application in with the Phoenix Police Department for several months, and I knew he was eager to move back to his hometown. Life in Lonesome Valley didn't hold the same appeal for the young man as it did for me.

"I take it you finally heard from the Phoenix PD?"

"Yep. I can't wait. Just three more weeks on the job here. I'm going to spend the next couple of days looking for an apartment in Phoenix. I can always stay with my parents for a while if I have to, but I'd rather not move twice. Besides, I'm almost positive that they're going to need their spare bedroom for my grandmother soon. She's seriously considering spending the winter in Phoenix with the family, instead of here in

Lonesome Valley. She likes it here, except for the cooler winters.

I nodded. "When I told my friends in Kansas City I was planning to move to Arizona, they all assumed it was hot here all the time, but they didn't realize that Northern Arizona's not like that, at least around here. In fact, it was snowing back in January, the day I moved into my house. I'm glad we don't get a lot of the white stuff in Lonesome Valley, though."

We turned the corner to Main Street and sat in the shade on one of the benches that the Lonesome Valley Downtown Merchants' Association had provided along Main Street.

"What did you want to talk to me about, Amanda?"

"The accident Sunday night out on the highway Were you on duty that night?"

"As a matter of fact, I was the first officer to arrive at the scene. An ambulance showed up about the same time, but I was able to talk to the driver before they transported him to the hospital. At first, I thought it was a single-vehicle accident, and the driver had swerved off the road and ended up in the ditch, maybe to avoid hitting an animal on the highway, but he told me someone had run into the back of his car and forced him off. Why did you want to know?"

"The driver's a famous artist. He was here for the opening of his one-man show at the new gallery in the resort, and he was also the feature attraction at a painting event and art auction last Saturday."

"A friend of yours?"

"More of an acquaintance, I'd say, but I wondered whether you knew that he's now in a coma."

"No, I hadn't heard. He didn't seem badly hurt when I questioned him at the scene. He didn't see the vehicle that hit him, but the driver who called 9-1-1 said a dark-colored pickup truck hit him. That's about all we have to go on. We put out an appeal via the news media, asking anyone else who might have witnessed the crash to come forward, but, so far, that hasn't happened. Unfortunately, the chances of finding the driver who hit him are low. We just don't have much to go on. I'll let Sergeant Martinez know about your friend's condition. I'm sure he'll get in touch with the hospital so we can keep tabs on the victim. If it turns out to be a fatal accident—"

I groaned.

"Oh, sorry, Amanda. I hope your artist friend will be all right. You don't happen to know what his prognosis is, do you?"

"No. At first, the doctor planned on releasing him the next day, but then he fell into a coma. Ulysses's wife Olivia is terribly upset."

"I understand."

"Do you check the local auto body shops to see if anyone's come in for repairs?"

"Sure do. That's routine with a hit-and-run accident. The truck that caused the accident's going to have some white paint on its front bumper. So far, no luck on that score, though, but we'll keep trying. I'm sorry we haven't been able to find the driver who caused the accident. These hit-and-run cases can be tough to crack. Whoever did it could be thousands of miles away by now."

Or right here in Lonesome Valley, I thought.

Chapter 15

"Let's go, Laddie," I urged, after I snapped on his collar and leash. "Mr. Big's waiting for you."

Laddie rushed out the door and spotted his little buddy and Belle waiting for us on the front sidewalk. He tugged at his leash in an effort to hurry me along.

"Looks like he's raring to go," Belle observed.

"He is, especially since we skipped his walk this morning, and he was home alone most of the day. Well, not really alone, but Mona Lisa's not much company for him."

Laddie and Mr. Big veered left, the direction we normally went on our way to the park, but Belle gently steered Mr. Big to the right.

"Let's go this way. I'm still trying to satisfy my curiosity about our new neighbor. I've noticed a couple of delivery trucks over there and a plumber, but I've yet to see any occupants."

The house next door didn't look much different to me than it had the last time Belle and I had passed by, but Belle pointed out that the shades in the front of the house looked different. We were both staring at the large picture window when the horizontal slats slowly descended to the sill and rotated until they totally blocked any view we might have had of the interior.

"I guess someone doesn't want their snoopy neighbors seeing inside." Belle chuckled.

"It almost looks like an automatic process, the way those blinds went down, like it's operated by remote control or something."

"Could be. Well, I guess whoever moved in there will have to come out eventually."

I hadn't really given the house a second thought since the last time we'd passed by. I only hoped my visitors' parking for my Friday night studio tour wouldn't become an issue. Tour visitors had been sparse the last couple of weeks, but occasionally several people showed up at about the same time. Belle didn't think it would be a problem, though, and I hoped she was right.

We circled the block and headed toward the park.

"Maybe we'll run into Rebecca and Greg," Belle said. "I haven't seen them since we got back from Michigan."

We'd met Rebecca and Greg Winter several months earlier, when they'd offered us a ride home after a jogger had collided with Belle and she'd sprained her ankle. Rebecca and Greg were pet parents to two small terriers, and Laddie and Mr. Big were always on the lookout for the lively pair whenever we walked in the park.

"Oh, I forgot to tell you. They're on vacation. Greg said he likes to wait until school's in session before they hit the road in their RV. They're planning on visiting some of the national parks. Rebecca told me they'd be gone about a month."

"They took the terriers with them, I suppose."

"Yes, Rebecca said they're good little travelers."

"I wish Mr. Big liked to travel. He's fine around town, but when we get out on the highway, he seems to sense it's going to be a long trip, and he gets so excited that it's hard to calm him down. But, of course, we wouldn't go visit the kids without him. Our grandchildren are just as happy to see him as they are to see us. He plays with them for hours on end."

We paused a minute while Belle checked Mr. Big's collar, and Laddie took the opportunity to roll in the grass. Once Belle released him, Mr. Big playfully bounced around Laddie until he reluctantly stood, and we continued on our way.

I told Belle what I'd learned from Mike about Ulysses's accident.

"So the police are looking for a dark-colored pickup truck with white paint on the front bumper. It doesn't seem like much to go on."

"No, it sure isn't. I don't think the likelihood of finding the hit-and-run driver is very high. At least, that's what Mike said. It just seems too coincidental to me, ending up in an accident when he was going to pick up his kidnapped wife, but that's not the only thing that's coincidental. Why did the kidnappers snatch Olivia during the plein air event? That smacks of a very deliberate action, like maybe somebody was trying to send Ulysses a message."

"How so?"

"I don't really know, but why choose that particular spot? It's almost as though kidnapping her wasn't enough, as though the kidnappers wanted to remind Ulysses of what happened the last time he went to a paint-out at Miners' Lookout."

"But who would know about that? Didn't you tell me Ulysses's first wife disappeared almost thirty years ago?"

"Right, according to Pamela."

"So other than Pamela and Ulysses, who's still around here who would remember it?"

"I assume Olivia probably knows what happened, although it's possible she doesn't. Maybe Ulysses never told her the story of how Jill left him. Then, there's Ralph, of course. He was Ulysses's teacher at the time, and he organized the paint-out."

"Ralph—isn't he the white-haired gentleman I met at the gallery when I came in to buy my cousin a birthday present a couple of months ago?"

"Yes, that's Ralph. He's one of the founders of the Roadrunner. I suppose he's lived in Lonesome Valley quite a while if he was teaching private art classes here so long ago."

"I don't remember seeing him at the auction."

"You're right. He wasn't there. He signed up to participate in the paint-out, but he didn't show up. His arthritis has been bothering him something terrible lately, so I'm sure that's the reason he couldn't come."

"Do you really think someone who held a grudge against Ulysses all those years ago might be behind Olivia's kidnapping?

"I don't know. That doesn't seem to make much sense, I guess. From what we know, the only person who might fit into that category is Ulysses's ex-wife Jill. You don't suppose—"

"Jill kidnapped Olivia? Seems pretty far-fetched to me. She doesn't live here in Lonesome Valley, does she?"

"Not as far as I know, but it might be interesting to find out. Maybe Pamela knows. I'm working at the gallery tomorrow afternoon. I could ask her."

"I'm working tomorrow afternoon, too—doing my volunteer stint at the library. I have an idea. We have all the old issues of the Lonesome Valley Chronicle on microfiche. It's not as easy to use as an online search, but I should have some time after Xena and I finish re-shelving books and tidying up the magazines. I can check to find out if anything was reported back then. You said a search was organized for Jill, right?"

"That's what Pamela told me. It must have been embarrassing for Ulysses when he found out Jill had left him, especially the way she did it."

"I'll see what I can dig up. Thirty years ago, right?"

"Pamela said twenty-eight, but I don't know the exact date. It must have been sometime in the summer because Pamela was in college then, and she was on her summer break."

"OK, I'll look into it. If the Chronicle's deadline came while the search was still on, there should be something about it in the paper. If not, the disappearance story might not have been reported, since Jill left of her own volition and no foul play was involved."

"All right. We might as well find out what we can."

"Agreed. We'll satisfy our curiosity, if nothing else. Why don't you come over for dinner tomorrow, and we can compare notes."

"Sounds good. I'll bring dessert."

"All the better, and bring Laddie with you, of course."

Wagging his tail, Laddie looked up at us when he heard his name, as though he knew just what we were talking about and approved heartily.

Unfortunately, he wasn't quite as happy when I left him the next day for my four-hour afternoon shift at the Roadrunner, but he was likely to spend most of the afternoon napping, so I told myself he wouldn't miss me too much because he'd be asleep,

Mid-week at the gallery wasn't likely to be too busy. Tour buses normally arrived on Fridays, and most tourists who drove themselves to Lonesome Valley favored weekends. Besides a refurbished historic downtown hotel and the swank Lonesome

Valley Resort, tourists had a wide choice of accommodations, including several motels along the highway and numerous bed-and-breakfast inns around town. Lonesome Valley catered to the out-of-towners who kept the economy humming. The Roadrunner and other shops and galleries downtown couldn't survive on local business alone, so we were very glad to welcome tourists and to participate in events that drew crowds to town.

When I arrived at the gallery shortly before one, several people were gathered at the jewelry counter. Carrie, one of our members who made jewelry, was holding up a counter mirror so that a woman who was trying on one of Carrie's turquoise necklaces could see how it looked on her.

The cash register separated the glass jewelry case from another counter that contained drawers beneath it. I pulled the bottom drawer open and deposited my handbag inside before signing in and noting the time I'd arrived.

Carrie moved over to the register to ring up her sale, and I carefully wrapped the lovely turquoise necklace in tissue paper, tucked it into a jewelry box, and placed it in one of the Roadrunner's signature bags.

"Nice sale, Carrie," I said, as the group of women headed for the door.

"Yes, great. I'm having a good month, and I'm starting to run low on inventory. I'm going home to finish the necklace I've been working on, so I can replace the one I sold. See you later."

Carrie was off with a spring in her step. She enjoyed steadier sales than most of the painters in the gallery. It probably helped that she had quite a few more affordable items, such as earrings, in her jewelry collection, in addition to her pricey necklaces.

Nobody else had signed in to work with me for the

afternoon, so I consulted the schedule to see who was due for the afternoon shift. Our policy was that there always had to be at least two members on duty at all times. A quick glance at the schedule answered my question. Ralph was supposed to work with me, but I hadn't seen him since the opening of Ulysses's show at the resort.

I was just about to walk back to the office to ask Pamela whether she'd heard from Ralph when she appeared.

"Ralph's not going to be able to come in again today," she told me, "so I'll fill in for him. I was planning on being here this afternoon, anyway."

Since Pamela and I were alone in the gallery, it seemed like the perfect time to find out more details about Jill's disappearance. I had to remind myself that Pamela knew nothing about Olivia's kidnapping and probably hadn't heard about Ulysses's accident, either. She was shocked when I told her he was in the ICU at Lonesome Valley Hospital and that he was in a coma.

"Poor Ulysses! What terrible luck!"

Pamela went pale and sat down on a stool that we kept behind the counter.

"Are you all right, Pamela?"

"Yes. I'm just so surprised. He was perfectly fine when he came in here the other day and now to think of him in a coma—it's awful."

I was beginning to get the feeling that Pamela knew Ulysses a little better than I'd realized.

"You must have been good friends when you were both Ralph's students."

"You could say that. I had a huge crush on Ulysses at the time. It was the summer before my junior year in college, and he paid a lot of attention to me. I suppose I was flattered because he was older and obviously the best student in Ralph's class. Everybody knew he was going places. I remember how thrilled I was when he asked me out. He took me to a lovely little restaurant, and the first thing he did was order us champagne. Just as he offered a toast "to us," Jill showed up. Of course, I didn't have a clue that he was married. He'd certainly never mentioned it. You can imagine what a scene she caused. She dragged him out of the restaurant, and there I was, all alone, with no way to get home. I didn't have a cell phone back then, so I had to ask the maître d' to use the restaurant's phone to call my brother for a ride home."

"How dreadful for you!"

"I was so humiliated I skipped Ralph's art class the next day, and I didn't go to the paint-out at Miners' Lookout that weekend, either. By the time I saw Ulysses again, he was a free man, or at least, he was about to be."

Chapter 16

"I went back to art class after the paint-out, and I felt relieved that Ulysses didn't come to class that day," Pamela said. "By the time he finally showed up a week later, I was still angry with him for not telling me he was married, but the word about how his wife had left him was out, and I suppose I harbored some hope that he'd turn to me, even though the other students who'd been at the plein air event had told me how upset he was when he thought she'd gone missing."

"What happened?"

"He didn't say a word to me or anybody else during class. We painted all morning, and he never left his easel. Ralph always made the rounds as we worked, encouraging us and giving us tips, but he didn't go near Ulysses that morning. Nobody tried to engage him in conversation. I suppose we all figured he wouldn't want to talk about what happened, so we gave him a wide berth. As I was leaving after class, Ulysses stopped me and told me that he would be getting a divorce from Jill and that he never would have asked me out if his marriage hadn't already been in trouble."

"And you believed him."

Pamela nodded. "I did at the time. I was young and naive,

and I was infatuated with him, despite what he'd done. So I agreed to go out with him again. We dated until our summer art classes with Ralph ended, and it was time for me to go back to ASU. Ulysses told me he was going to Mexico to get his divorce and then he'd join me in Phoenix. I heard from him a few times that fall, but he never came back here—not to Phoenix and not to Lonesome Valley—until a few weeks ago."

"Were you upset?"

"Devastated at the time, but when he didn't show up by Christmas, I finally realized he had no intention of coming back. A few months later, I met Rich. He was a grad student at the time. We got married right after my graduation about a year later."

"Did you stay in contact with any of the others from your summer art class?"

"Ralph, of course. I've always looked on him as a mentor. I've also stayed in touch with a couple of sisters who teach art in Florida, but I have no idea what became of the rest of them. We were all quite serious about our art, so I wouldn't be surprised if several of them made a career out of it. I confess I've followed Ulysses's career all these years. I don't really know why. Curiosity about the one who got away, I suppose."

We were both turned toward the gallery's large plate glass windows facing Main Street so that we could be on the lookout for potential customers when we spotted Marie, the owner of the Coffee Klatsch next door, headed our way. We greeted her as she opened the door, and I immediately went over to the jewelry counter to unlock it. Marie was a regular customer, just as the artists from the Roadrunner were regular customers of hers. We often popped next door for a caffeine-laden pick-me-up.

"Hi, girls," she said, although it had been decades since either Pamela or I had been a girl. "What's new?"

"You're in luck," I told her. "Half of the jewelry in this case has been brought in since you were here last."

"Be sure to check out the art glass pieces," Pamela said. "Our newest member makes both jewelry and glass sculptures."

Marie moved to the jewelry counter and peered inside. Meanwhile, I removed several carded pairs of earrings for her to look at. Her eclectic taste made it easy for us to accommodate her. Whenever she came into gallery, she always purchased at least one item of jewelry. Occasionally, she'd wander through the gallery, looking at the paintings on display, but she always returned to the jewelry case in the end. When she looked at the earrings I'd placed atop a black velvet cloth on the counter, she immediately picked up a pair of unique red and turquoise braided leather earrings with sterling silver French wires.

"Mind if I try these on?" she asked.

"Of course not. Let me grab the mirror." I hauled out our flexible mirror, set it on top of the counter and tilted it so that she could see her reflection. She took off the sparkly chandelier earrings she was wearing and put on the braided leather ones. She cupped her hands behind her ears, giving the two-inch long braided dangles a slight tap so that they swayed back and forth.

"I'll take these," she said as she took them off and slipped the wire hooks back onto the earring card. I set the earrings aside and returned the others I'd pulled out to the case as she continued to peer inside.

"Anything else catch your eye?"

"Yes, that pendant necklace there." She pointed to a large art glass pendant hung on a sturdy cord. The colorful abstract design of the large teardrop-shaped pendant reminded me of one of my tie-dyed scarves. I recognized the necklace as the work of our newest member, and I felt sure she'd be happy if any of her jewelry sold the first week it was on display. I reached into the case and carefully removed the necklace, setting it gently on the black velvet cloth so that Marie could look at it more closely. I wasn't surprised when she decided to try it on, since it made such a distinctive fashion statement, but I was a bit surprised when she decided to buy it, too, mainly because she usually limited her purchases to earrings.

I rang up the sale while Pamela carefully wrapped and packaged Marie's jewelry. Marie folded her receipt around her credit card, tucked it into her wallet, and dropped her wallet into her purse. With a smile, Pamela handed Marie her bagged jewelry.

"Be still my heart! Three beauties are gracing our gallery today."

I looked up to see Chip holding his hand over his heart and grinning at us. He hadn't come in the front door, so I supposed he'd been working in the apartment upstairs, which he used as his studio. Although he could have lived in the apartment, too, he preferred to stay at home with his parents, where his mother indulged him, although I knew his father, who expected Chip to show up promptly for work at his pizza parlor, did not. Delivering pizza may not have been the most exciting job in the world for the budding artist, but his job didn't take so much time that he couldn't work on his art. Still, despite loads of encouragement from Susan, his progress had been marked by fits and starts. Sometimes, he was productive; other times, he didn't pick up a paint brush for weeks. When I'd first joined the gallery, not a single painting of Chip's had been on display, despite the fact that he was a member of the gallery's board of directors, but since then he'd hung a few paintings and

completed a mural covering an entire wall in our mee
room, so maybe he was making some progress.

"Yes, aren't you the lucky one?" Marie said flirtatiou
giving Chip a wink.

"Indeed, I am."

Pamela and I looked at each other. Chip and Pamela
had a brief fling a few months earlier. It was over, l
evidently, neither harbored any ill will toward the other.
never told Pamela that Chip had offered to break up with
if I would agree to go out with him, which I'd never had
slightest intention of doing, but I think she'd come to rea
that he was a bit fickle, to say the least. At the time, Pame
husband had seldom been at home, and she was feeling lo
and neglected, but ever since Rich had moved his business f
Phoenix to Lonesome Valley, things had changed, and Pan
no longer complained that she was alone most of the time.

"What can I do for you, fair lady, on this lovely day?" C
asked Marie.

"You can come over to the Coffee Klatsch so that I can sl
you which wall to paint."

"Your wish is my command," he said with a bow. "I'l
right over as soon as I take care of some gallery business."

"Don't be long."

"I won't. I promise."

"Chip, you're incorrigible. I hope you're not going to I
Marie on," I said.

"Who me? No such thing. I'm just being friendly."

"Uh, huh."

Pamela ignored this exchange. She came out from beh
the counter and said, "Tell me you're going to paint a mur
the Coffee Klatsch."

"That's exactly what I plan to do." He reached into the pocket of his jeans to pull out a piece of paper. He unfolded it, smoothed it, and spread it out on the top of the counter. "I have something like this in mind, if Marie approves." He moved the sketch sideways so that both Pamela and I would be able to see it. It depicted an outdoor scene with customers seated at tiny tables on the Coffee Klatsch's patio, enjoying coffee while a server stood by with a large pot of the Klatsch's signature brew.

"I'm sure Marie will love it," I said. "It's really spot on."

Chip looked pleased at my assessment. He glanced at Pamela for her approval.

"What do you think?"

"I agree with Amanda. It's perfect for the Coffee Klatsch. Has Marie definitely hired you to paint the mural?"

"Not yet, but if you two think this is good, I'll head over there right now and seal the deal."

Chip planted an enthusiastic kiss on Pamela's cheek, just as Rich opened the door. Unfazed by the entrance of Pamela's husband, he extended his hand to shake Rich's. Rich made no move to shake hands, though, and the two stared at each other for an awkward moment until Rich broke the silence.

"Just what do you think you're doing?" Rich demanded.

"Nothing. I'm just going about my business."

"You leave my wife alone. If I ever see you touch her again, I'll make sure you regret it."

Chip shrugged, circled around Rich, and walked out the door.

"Rich, honestly, was that really necessary? Chip was just showing Amanda and me plans for a mural he's going to paint next door."

Chapter 17

The second I heard the office door open, I crouched behind the jewelry counter and busied myself with rearranging necklaces on the bottom shelf. When Rich stormed past the counter on his way to the gallery door, he didn't notice me. Mission accomplished, I thought, as I closed the case and stood up. At least, I'd managed to stay out of his way.

Half an hour later, there were no customers in the gallery, and Pamela still hadn't come out of her office. I walked down the hall toward her office. Seeing that her door was open, I knocked on the frame before stepping inside.

"Are you all right, Pamela?"

"I will be," she said, dropping a tissue into the wastebasket beside her desk. "I'm sorry you had to witness that scene. Rich can be so—"

"Jealous?"

She nodded, took another tissue from the box on her desk, and delicately dabbed at her red-rimmed eyes.

"He's not always like this, Amanda, but Chip set him off."

"Does he know about you and Chip?"

"He suspects, but that's been over for months. If Rich hadn't been away from home so much back then, I never would have started seeing Chip. What am I going to do, Amanda? He's demanding that I resign as gallery director so that I won't see Chip here."

"Oh, no. You're not seriously considering resigning, are you?"

"I'm afraid I am. I don't want to lose my husband."

I heard the gallery door open, so I stepped out into the hall to see who had come in. Chip rushed in, carrying three large cups from the Coffee Klatsch in a cardboard container. He saw me and came down the hall, entering Pamela's office, where he deposited the cardboard container on her desktop. She had turned her face so that, at first, he didn't notice that she was upset.

"I come bearing gifts. Well, coffee, anyway, to celebrate," Chip said, as he handed me a mocha. "Marie hired me to paint the mural for the Coffee Klatsch. I showed her the sketch, and she really likes my idea."

"That's great, Chip! Congratulations!" I said. "Let's go back into the gallery, and you can tell me all about it."

"But I want to tell Pamela, too," he said, looking her way and finally realizing that she was distressed. "What's wrong, Pamela? Don't tell me your husband gave you a hard time over a little kiss."

"He did. He wants me to avoid you."

"But that's impossible when we're both here so much of the time."

"Exactly. He wants me to resign as gallery director."

"Don't resign! I think he's being unreasonable, but I don't have to use the apartment upstairs as my studio. I can work at Aunt Susan's. She has plenty of extra room, and I know she won't mind."

"I don't want to put you out."

"You're not putting me out. I can switch my gallery work days to the days you're not here."

"But we're both on the board."

"I'll resign from the board."

"Oh, Chip," Pamela sniffed.

"I don't want to be the cause of any problems for you. Won't he be satisfied if we don't see each other?"

"I suppose so."

"Well, do your best to persuade him, because I don't want you to be forced into giving up the gallery directorship. I know how much it means to you."

Chip was right about that. Pamela loved being the director of the Roadrunner, and she was very good at her job. I wondered whether Rich would consider the concessions Chip offered as satisfactory, or whether he would renew his demand that she resign.

"Well, if you're sure . . . ."

"I am. Now have your macchiato and try to relax for a while. I'm going to go look at our work schedule and arrange to trade times."

Luckily, we hadn't had any customers come into the gallery during all the drama. I followed Chip back into the gallery, leaving Pamela to pull herself together. Chip went straight to the counter, pulled out the top drawer, and rummaged through it.

"Do you know where the schedule book is, Amanda? We always used to keep it in the top drawer."

"It should be there. Let me take a look. Maybe somebody moved it."

After searching through a couple of other drawers, I finally found it under a stack of bags.

"Here it is," I held up the spiral-bound notebook on the counter and opened it to the September schedule. "No idea how it ended up there," I muttered.

"Thanks. Let's take a look." Chip scanned the month's schedule. "If I trade days with Valerie, that should take care of it. I'll give her a call."

He pulled his cell phone out of his pocket, then returned it just as quickly. He grinned. "Better wait till she's out of class. Don't worry, Amanda. I'll take care of this."

I nodded. "I really hope Pamela can work things out with Rich. You're right about how much being gallery director means to her."

Chip took another look at the notebook. "Let me double check the schedule for a back-up. It looks like I could switch with Carrie if Valerie's not able to do it. By the way, where's Ralph? According to this, he's supposed to be here with you this afternoon."

"He called Pamela and told her he wasn't able to make it today because his arthritis is kicking up again."

"Poor guy. I think I'll stop by his place to check on him while I'm out doing my deliveries this evening, maybe take him a pizza."

"That would be a nice gesture. I'm sure he would appreciate it."

"I'm just a nice guy," Chip said, reverting to his usual flirtatious behavior. He gave me an exaggerated wink along with a silly grin.

Saying that he had to go to work early, Chip left the gallery. Pamela didn't come out of her office the rest of the afternoon. Although we had a few customers, it wasn't busy, and I handled what little business we had on my own. Promptly at five, I went back to the office and told Pamela I was leaving for the day.

"So am I," she said. "I guess I'll have to face the music sometime."

"Good luck," I told her, as she locked the gallery door. "I hope your husband changes his mind about your resigning."

"I think he might if he's satisfied that Chip won't be hanging around the gallery. I don't know what's gotten into him lately. He never used to be so jealous. Except once, but that was so long ago. See you later, Amanda."

Knowing how crowded the store would be, I debated whether or not to stop at the supermarket on the way home. Instead, I decided against it. Rather than making the pecan pie I'd planned on before remembering I had no pecans, I figured I would use whatever ingredients I had on hand to make a different pie to take to Belle's tonight.

Both Laddie and Mona Lisa rushed me as soon as I came in, and I devoted a few minutes to giving them hugs and cuddles before I opened the fridge and scanned the contents of my cupboards in search of ingredients for a pie. I always kept the basics on hand as well as a few frozen pie shells, so all I needed to do was settle on my pie filling. The bag of Granny Smith apples I'd bought a few days earlier made the decision easy, so I began peeling and slicing them until I had enough to fill a pie shell. I'd decided on a Dutch apple pie, rather than a traditional double-crust pie, so I combined the ingredients for the crumble topping and then assembled the pie.

I set the timer on the stove before giving Laddie and Mona Lisa their dinners. Then I went outside with Laddie. He wandered around while I sat in the shade on the patio. I was checking the weather forecast on my phone when Brooks called.

"Amanda, I've reported Olivia's kidnapping to the police," he said without preamble. "I thought about what you said, and you're right. Whoever's behind the kidnapping could strike again. I thought I should give you a heads-up because I'm sure the police will be getting in touch with you."

"All right. Thanks for letting me know. I'm a little surprised. You seemed to be against the idea of notifying the police when I saw you yesterday."

"Yes, well. Let's just say I've thought better of it, even though Olivia and Gabrielle didn't want me to do it."

I could understand the reason Olivia might not want to endure a police interrogation after her ordeal and now her worry about Ulysses's condition, but I had no idea why Gabrielle hadn't wanted Brooks to report the kidnapping to the police. Perhaps she didn't want the hassle of answering questions, but I knew she couldn't avoid that. The police were sure to talk to everybody who'd been at the paint-out on Saturday when Olivia had disappeared. I had no idea what the chances were of the police finding the kidnapper, but I was hoping they had a better shot at it than they did of finding the driver who had run Ulysses off the road.

My apple pie was still warm when Laddie and I approached Belle's front door an hour later. The door swung open before we went up the front steps, and Mr. Big ran outside to greet us. Belle called him back inside, and he complied, but then he ran back out to Laddie. I carefully stepped around him so that I wouldn't trip over the excited little dog.

"I'll set the pie on the counter," Belle said, taking the box I'd put the pie in. "It smells so good. I haven't had apple pie for ages. We have some French vanilla ice cream that would be perfect with it."

"That sounds good. I should have thought to pick up some ice cream on my way home, but I hadn't actually decided which dessert to make yet."

"I thought I heard a commotion," Dennis said, stepping into the kitchen from the patio.

Laddie jumped up and down at the sight of Dennis because he knew Dennis would play fetch with him. Mr. Big loved to run along with Laddie while he retrieved the ball Dennis threw for him, although the little fluffy dog didn't have any retriever genes and wasn't interested in fetching anything.

"I'll grill the hamburgers as soon as I'm done supervising doggie playtime," Dennis said, as the dogs raced outside, ahead of him.

"Were you able to find out anything?" Belle asked.

"Not much. According to Pamela, she and Ralph are the only painters who still live here. I did find out that Ulysses was a player back then, though. His wife caught him when he was on a date with Pamela, and she left him not long after."

"Do you think that's the reason Jill left him?"

"It could be, although Ulysses later told Pamela that they'd been having problems for a while. I don't know if that's true or not. It's possible he said that to convince her to go out with him after Jill left, though. How did you fare at the library? Was there anything in the paper back then about Jill's disappearance?"

"A couple of articles. I made copies. Just a second. They're still in my bag."

Belle retrieved the printed copies of the the articles and set them out on the kitchen table.

"The first one says that searchers are looking for a missing woman in the area around Miners' Lookout. That hit the front page with a couple of photos. Of course, that's all the reporter knew when the Chronicle went to press. By the time the newspaper was delivered the next morning, Ulysses knew his wife had left him. The second article was very short and ran on page six, just saying that the missing woman had been located. There were no other details."

I stared at the grainy pictures that accompanied the first article. One was a photo of a very young-looking Jill.

"Do you suppose that's her college graduation picture?" I asked.

Belle took a closer look. "I don't know. She looks so young. I think it might be her high school graduation photo."

I peered more carefully at the other picture that accompanied the story. It showed a small group of searchers at Miners' Lookout. It wasn't very clear, but one of the searchers looked vaguely familiar. I had to keep in mind that he would be nearly thirty years older now, but the more I stared at the picture, the more confident I became that I recognized him.

The man in the Chronicle's photo, one of a team of searchers, looked quite like the grumpy police detective who'd arrested my friend Susan for murder a few months earlier and implied that he suspected me, too. It was none other than my nemesis Lieutenant Belmont.

Chapter 18

Tempted as I was to learn more details about the search for Jill decades ago, Lieutenant Belmont was the last person I wanted to ask for information. Still, my curiosity was pushing me to talk to him, even though my better judgment told me not to do it.

It was easy to defer a decision, though, since I planned to spend the next day in my studio, and I'd resolved not to become sidetracked again. The two pet portraits and my latest landscape beckoned me to finish them, and I was further spurred on by the prospect of collecting the last half of the payments due me on completion of the pet portraits.

After an early morning walk in the park with Laddie and a light breakfast of tea and toast, I went to work in the studio. As always, Laddie followed me. There wasn't much for him to do while I painted, so he curled up on his doggy bed in the corner of the studio and snoozed.

I'd been painting for a couple hours, and I was very close to completing the final touches on my painting of the two Siamese cats when Laddie jumped up and ran to the kitchen door, his tail sweeping back and forth as he wagged it in eager anticipation. I set my brush down and followed him. Before I could reach the door, Belle knocked. I could always tell it was Belle when she knocked with her usual three sharp staccato raps.

"Come in," I invited her, swinging the door open. She had her hands full, so I held Laddie back for a few seconds, long enough for Belle to set the cake she'd brought on the kitchen counter. As soon as she put it down, she called Laddie over and petted him.

"The last of the dates," she said, waving her hand in the direction of the counter. "I had just enough to make us each a cake. It's a recipe handed down from my grandmother, and it's really yummy. I know you'll like it."

"I'm sure I will. How about some coffee? We can sample the cake right now."

"I wish I had time, but I'm off to a dental appointment. I won't be eating much of anything until later today."

"I don't envy you," I said, shuddering. Briefly, I wondered which I would most like to avoid—going to the dentist or talking to Lieutenant Belmont. I decided it would be pretty much a toss-up. "I hope it doesn't take long at the dentist. We can have a tasting whenever you feel up to it."

I took time to drink another cup of tea before returning to the studio. Laddie trailed along and settled himself on his bed again. To my surprise, Mona Lisa made an appearance, too. She circled the studio, switched her tail at Laddie as she passed by him, and ignored me completely. Her exploration complete, she looked back at us with disdain and went back into the living room. No doubt she'd want to get chummy with me later. There was no accounting for my cat's strange mood swings.

Returning to my painting of the Siamese cat duo, I finished the final detail work and carefully added my artist's signature at the bottom right.

I set my brush down and stepped back from my painting. Pleased with the results, I picked up my digital camera to take a picture, which I'd send to the buyers with my final invoice. When I pressed the "on" button, nothing happened, and I knew I'd have to replace the batteries. It seemed like the camera ate them, I had to replace them so often. My camera took two double A batteries. I rummaged around in the top drawer, where I kept batteries, and came up with only one. Since I didn't want to interrupt my work session to run to the store, I decided to press on with the other portrait and leave the shopping until later.

I was returning the lone battery to the drawer when Laddie jumped up again. His time, he stationed himself at the front door. His tail swept back and forth, but more slowly than it had when he was expecting Belle. Laddie loved company, and he was friendly to everybody, but I could always tell if he knew the person on the other side of the door by the velocity of his wagging tail.

I opened the door and was shocked to find Lieutentant Belmont standing on my doorstep. I was even more shocked when he greeted Laddie with "hey, there, fella," and reached out a hand to scratch behind my affable retriever's ears. Of course, Laddie basked in the attention. Little did he know that, in all my previous encounters with Lieutenant Belmont, the man had been either accusatory or dismissive toward me.

"I'd like to ask you some questions, if you don't mind."

The lieutenant looked as rumpled as usual in an ill-fitting suit and wrinkled shirt. Beads of perspiration dotted his forehead.

"All right." I opened the door wider so that he could enter. Waving him toward the sofa, I took a seat in the armchair opposite him while Laddie sat in front of me with his ears perked up.

I couldn't help but notice that the lieutenant looked supremely uncomfortable as he removed a small notebook and pen from his jacket pocket. He looked around the room and muttered "nice house."

"Thank you."

I almost fell out of my chair. The lieutenant seemed to be making a concerted effort to be pleasant, something I'd never known him to do before, but I found it difficult to believe that he'd suddenly turned over a new leaf.

"Brooks told me he'd reported Olivia Durand's kidnapping to the police. Is that what you wanted to ask me about?"

"Uh, yes. Mr. Miller reported it to the chief."

I was beginning to get the drift. From the way the lieutenant said Brooks's name, I could tell that he regarded him as some sort of authority. Brooks had gone directly to the chief, the lieutenant's boss, rather than through normal channels. Perhaps the chief had warned the lieutenant to treat the witnesses with kid gloves. I wouldn't put it past Brooks to use his considerable influence to make that happen. Maybe this wouldn't be so bad after all.

The lieutenant cleared his throat and asked me first whether I'd noticed Olivia leaving the paint-out and next about my delivery of the ransom.

I told him I hadn't really paid attention to much besides my painting during the plein air event, so I hadn't noticed Olivia's absence until Ulysses did. Then I related the story of my involvement and how I'd delivered the ransom, following exactly the instructions the kidnapper had given Ulysses. While I talked, the lieutenant jotted down a few notes, but he didn't interrupt me. I'd been leaning forward in my chair and petting Laddie while I told the lieutenant my story. When I was done, I sank back in the plush chair.

Sensing that he was losing my attention, Laddie went over to the lieutenant and stood in front of him, looking up hopefully. The lieutenant put his notebook and pen down on the side table next to him and obliged my furry pet by scratching behind his ears again.

"What's his name?"

"Laddie," I answered. I didn't want to say too much. So far, so good. I found it hard to believe that he was a dog lover, but he certainly wouldn't be accommodating my pet if he weren't.

"Well, you're a good boy, Laddie."

"Yes, he is," I said. "He's a great dog." I almost asked him if he had any more questions before realizing I'd never get a better opportunity to ask some questions of my own. "Would you like some coffee, lieutenant? I was just about to put some on before you came." That was a fib, but it sounded reasonable. I wasn't a big coffee drinker, but I liked the specialty drinks at the Coffee Klatsch, and I occasionally drank regular coffee at home, too. The lieutenant couldn't possibly know that my go-to drink was tea, though, so he shouldn't find my claim unusual. Even so, I was a bit surprised when he took me up on my offer.

I walked the few feet to my tiny kitchen to put the pot on. When I saw the lieutenant eyeing the cake Belle had left on the counter, I immediately offered him a piece, and he didn't waste any time accepting.

"How do you take your coffee, lieutenant? Milk? Sugar?"

"Just black."

I poured the steaming coffee into a mug, set a wool rug mug on the table beside him, and carefully put the coffee down. I returned to the kitchen and cut him a generous slice of cake. Putting a dessert fork, tines down, on the plate, so it would be less likely to tumble off, I grabbed a couple napkins and set one under the plate and the other beside it as I placed it next to the coffee mug I'd given him. Then, I grabbed myself half a cup of coffee and some cake.

I was about to join the lieutenant when Laddie came over to me and whimpered softly. I knew he was after a treat for himself, so I obliged him, putting a few baby carrots in his bowl. By the time I returned to the living room, the lieutenant's plate was empty.

"Would you like another slice of cake?" If I didn't stall, I was afraid he'd leave before I could ask him about Jill's long-ago disappearance. Then all my buttering-up efforts would go for naught.

Luckily, he accepted my offer. There didn't seem to be a good way to approach the subject, and I realized he probably wouldn't tell me anything, but I figured it was now or never.

"Olivia's kidnapping must remind you of Ulysses's first wife's disappearance."

"How do you know about that?" he asked sharply. Laddie had been headed back toward him, but as soon as he heard the lieutenant's tone, he veered off course and came to me.

"He's very sensitive," I told the lieutenant.

"I can see that." He clucked softly and patted his leg.

"It's OK, Laddie," I assured him, and with that, he trotted over to his new buddy.

"What is it you want to know, Mrs. Trent?"

Chapter 19

"It struck me as odd that Olivia was kidnapped from the same place and at a similar event where Ulysses's first wife disappeared, so I thought perhaps the kidnappers might have been at the first paint-out or known what happened there. Maybe they planned the kidnapping in the same place to goad Ulysses."

"Seems a little far-fetched to me," Lieutenant Belmont said. "I figure whoever did it heard a rich guy was in town and saw an opportunity to make some money by grabbing his wife."

"But why there? Why at Miners' Lookout?"

The lieutenant shrugged. "Like I said, a crime of opportunity. The kidnappers could have been among the spectators."

"I suppose, but it seems so coincidental. I can't help thinking the two incidents are connected somehow." Then I had another, much darker thought. "Has anybody heard from Jill since she left Ulysses? What if she didn't really leave him? What if he's responsible for her disappearance?"

"One of your wild theories panned out once, so you think you're Miss Marple now, is that it?"

Same old lieutenant, I thought, but I could tell he knew

something, and he seemed eager to show me the error of my ways.

"I hate to disillusion you, but you're wrong," he continued. "Jill Durand really did leave her husband that day, although I'll admit it looked bad for Durand for a while."

The lieutenant tugged at his collar. I noticed beads of perspiration had popped out on his face, which had turned pale all of a sudden, though I had my air conditioning turned on, and the house felt quite cool.

"I don't feel so good," he moaned, clutching his chest.

He slumped over on the sofa, but he didn't try to swing his legs up. His breathing seemed labored, but, at least, he *was* breathing.

"Chest pain?"

Grimacing, he nodded.

I reached for my phone and punched in 9-1-1.

I was sure the lieutenant was having a heart attack, and he obviously knew it, too, because he didn't protest. Laddie stayed by his side as we awaited the arrival of an ambulance. I ran outside to flag the paramedics down as soon as I heard the siren. The two paramedics—a young woman and an older man—quickly assessed the situation as I held Laddie back so that they could check the lieutenant. As I'd expected, they rapidly made the decision to transport him to the hospital. He was able to move onto the gurney they'd brought in, which I thought might be a good sign.

"I'm sorry we're not permitted to let you ride along in the ambulance," the young paramedic told me, "but you'll be able to see your husband in the emergency room at the hospital."

"Oh, no, he's not my hus—" I began, but they were already out the door and beyond earshot.

When I sat down and gave Laddie a big hug, I realized I was shaking. It wasn't every day someone had a heart attack in my living room. After I recovered a bit, I realized I should notify the police department that Lieutenant Belmont had been taken to the hospital.

As luck would have it, Sergeant Martinez, whose wife Dawn was a member of the Roadrunner, was on duty. He knew why Lieutenant Belmont had come to my house, so there was no need for explanations.

"Thanks for letting us know, Amanda. I'll notify the chief and get the word out to the guys. He doesn't have any family, not around here, anyway, so I'll go check on him during my lunch break. I always said the guy was a heart attack waiting to happen. He never met a steak or a hamburger he didn't like, and he never got a lick of exercise. Too bad, though. I wouldn't wish a heart attack on my worst enemy."

Feeling guilty for tempting Lieutenant Belmont with cake, I worried that eating the sweet snack might have triggered his heart attack, but from what Sergeant Martinez had told me, it sounded as though Lieutenant Belmont had been building up to it for years.

I felt a bit unnerved, too. Whenever I became distracted, I couldn't concentrate on my painting. I realized that sometimes I'd rationalize not working, because I had a bad habit of procrastinating, but today wasn't one of those times. I truly needed to take a break and calm myself down after witnessing a guest's unexpected heart attack in my home.

"Let's go play fetch, Laddie."

Laddie deserved some extra play time. My canine companion had been a perfect gentleman while the paramedics were in the house. He'd stayed with the lieutenant while I ran outside to flag down the ambulance, and I'd noticed that the lieutenant had been resting his hand on Laddie's back when I led the paramedics into the house.

Laddie delighted in running to fetch his hard rubber ball and rushing back to me with it so that we could repeat the process over and over. Inevitably, I tired of the game before he did, and after half an hour of strenuous play, I insisted that we settle ourselves in the shade on the patio until we cooled down. By the time Laddie stopped panting, I was ready for a quick lunch, so we went inside where I rustled up a sandwich for myself and some carrots for Laddie.

Mona Lisa finally made her appearance as I was dropping the carrots into Laddie's bowl. She'd been hiding under my bed all morning. If I hadn't known her better, I would have been worried that she might be feeling sick, but since she often hid under the bed for hours at a time, I wasn't concerned. My calico kitty pounced on my feet and emitted a loud "meow." She'd seen me give Laddie a snack, and she wanted one, too. I obliged her, giving her a treat, and she seemed satisfied. As soon as she finished eating it, she leaped to the top of her kitty tree, where she kept a watchful eye on Laddie and me.

I was about ready to return to the studio and get back to my painting when Dawn called. "Hi, Amanda, I thought I'd give you an update on Bill."

I wondered who Bill was before it occurred to me that she must be referring to Lieutenant Belmont.

"When Dave called to tell me about Bill's heart attack, I insisted on meeting him at the hospital during his lunch hour. Bill's all alone. He doesn't have any family, and the guys at the station aren't exactly touchy feely. Most of them wouldn't have a clue what to say to him. They don't like him much, either.

Dave's about the only cop who gets along with Bill. Anyway, when we got there, the doctor told us the bad news."

"You mean . . . ."

"Oh, sorry, Amanda. I shouldn't have put it that way. Bill's alive, but the heart attack was very serious, according to his doctor. We were able to see him for a few minutes. The doctor recommended bypass surgery, but he wants to wait a few days to give Bill's heart time to recover from the attack. I know he's scared, but he tried to make light of it. He asked me to thank you for getting help so promptly."

"Of course. I'm not too well versed on emergency medical situations, but it was pretty obvious he was in trouble."

"Bill's resting comfortably now, as they say, but he'll be off work for several weeks. The chief's already tasked Dave with covering the lieutenant's cases."

"Thanks for letting me know, Dawn."

"I wonder if I could ask you a favor."

"Sure, what is it?" I fully expected Dawn to ask me to cover for her at the Roadrunner.

"Dave and I can't go by the hospital this evening. Our son's the starting pitcher for tonight's city league ball game. Could you stop by the hospital to check on Bill? You wouldn't need to stay long, but I'd feel better if someone looked in on him."

"Sure, Dawn. I can do that."

"He was such a bear to you a few months ago that I know it's asking a lot."

"It's not a problem. Really." I still felt somewhat guilty for plying the lieutenant with cake in hopes that he'd answer my questions. Even though I didn't look forward to my third visit to Lonesome Valley Hospital in only a few days, and I wasn't sure what kind of reception I'd get from the lieutenant, I felt obligated. And as Dawn said, I only needed to stay a few minutes.

Late that afternoon, I called Belle to find out whether she'd recovered from her dental appointment and to tell her the scoop. She asked me whether our new neighbor had made an appearance to see what was happening when the ambulance arrived, but I hadn't noticed any neighbors gathered to gawk. Most of them would have been at work that time of the day. As far as I knew, Belle and I were the only ones on our block who typically were home during the day.

"Wait till I tell Dennis you're actually going to visit Belmont in the hospital. He's not going to believe it."

Dennis had a low opinion of Lieutenant Belmont. They had both been members of a photography club, but Lieutenant Belmont had been so unpleasant that the members had voted to expel him. In retaliation, the lieutenant had taken every opportunity to write them tickets for minor infractions whenever he could.

I wasn't exactly looking forward to my hospital visit, but I'd promised Dawn I would do it. When the time came, I steeled myself for the journey. I wasn't exactly dreading it, but I wasn't sure that Lieutenant Belmont would appreciate the gesture.

It didn't seem right to visit a patient without taking some flowers or a snack. The lieutenant didn't appear to be the flowers type, and the last snack I'd given him certainly hadn't done him much good.

As soon as I came into the hospital's lobby, I headed straight for the gift shop, although I had no idea what to buy for a grumpy man who probably wouldn't be too pleased to see me, anyway.

While Xena was busy at the cash register, processing a

transaction, I couldn't help but noticing that my scarf display looked depleted. I made a quick count. There were eight scarves left on the display rack. When I'd sold the display to Xena on Tuesday, she'd bought a dozen.

After her customer left, Xena noticed me checking out the display.

"Hi, Amanda. You must be a mind reader. I was about to call you to order some more scarves."

"Oh, wow; that's great! I actually came in to find a little gift for a patient, but tell me how many scarves you need."

"We've sold four already. I'll be conservative and say six for now. Assorted colors will be fine."

"All right. I don't have that many in stock, but I can make more over the weekend and bring them in on Monday."

"Perfect. I won't be here that day, but I'll leave a check for you. Maybe I can help you find a gift for your friend."

"He's not really a friend, so I don't know what to take him, but I'd hate to show up empty-handed."

I explained enough about the situation for her to get the drift.

"How about a plant? It would last longer than flowers, and he could take it home when he's discharged. I have one here that looks good and doesn't require much care. With a weekly light watering, it should do well."

"All right. I guess that'll work."

"I can put a nice bow around it to make it look cheerier." She pointed to a stack of ribbons behind the counter. "Blue OK?"

"That's fine."

I watched as she made a bow. She threaded the ribbon around the foil on the potted plant and deftly attached the bow to it with a thin wire.

"How's that?"

"It looks good."

I felt awkward about taking Lieutenant Belmont a gift, which he'd probably hate, anyway, but as I paid for my purchase, I remembered Dawn's words. As she'd said, I wouldn't have to stay long.

"We water all the plants on Monday, so it won't need a drink for a few days yet."

"Thanks, Xena, and thanks for your order. I'll bring the scarves the first thing Monday morning."

I'd forgotten to ask Dawn the number of the lieutenant's room, so I stopped at the reception desk to get it before hopping on the elevator. Room 402 turned out to be at the end of a hallway, far away from the fourth floor nursing station. The door was wide open, but I didn't go in, because I could hear voices coming from the room.

"You can't expect me to eat this stuff," the lieutenant complained. "It's absolutely tasteless."

"Your doctor ordered a heart-healthy diet for you."

The lieutenant groaned. "If my heart doesn't kill me, this food will."

"I know it's not what you're used to, but try to eat a little. You'll get used to it."

"Hmpf! I doubt it."

The nurse left him to his own devices and bustled past me to continue her rounds.

Hesitantly, I rapped a couple times on the door frame to let the lieutenant know someone was coming.

As soon as he saw me, he scowled. Then, the scowl disappeared as though he'd thought of an idea.

"I don't suppose I could talk you into running over to the Burger Palace and getting me a triple cheeseburger and some fries?"

Chapter 20

"I don't suppose you could," I said, setting the plant down on the window ledge next to his bed. "I heard what the nurse said. You're supposed to be on a special diet."

"Just look at what they call a meal." He lifted the lid off his plate, revealing some baked fish, green beans, and zucchini. There was a bowl of salad next to his dinner plate. He held up a white packet. "Salt substitute! They won't even let me have real salt," he lamented.

I didn't comment. I could understand that he liked all the food that his doctor had forbidden. I wouldn't be happy if my doctor ordered me to cut out dessert, but if I had to do it for health reasons, I'd comply. I wasn't so sure about the lieutenant.

He gave me a canny look. "Tell you what, Mrs. Trent. You do me a favor, and I'll do you one. It'll take only a few minutes for you to run over to the Burger Palace, and when you come back with my cheeseburger and fries, I'll tell you everything I know about Durand."

"No way. The nurses would stop me as soon as I got off the elevator. Besides, it's for your own good. You need to take care of yourself so you can get well."

"Oh, all right," he said sulkily, as I turned to leave. "Wait a minute." He grabbed the remote control and pointed it toward the portable TV set on the wall opposite his bed.

The sound hadn't been on, and I hadn't noticed the TV earlier. He zapped the set off, and the picture disappeared. He motioned toward a chair beside his hospital bed.

"Sit down, Mrs. Trent," he said. "I'll tell you what I know. You're such a snoop you probably won't leave me in peace until I do. Anyway, there's nothing on the television."

As I sat down, I wondered how seriously he was taking his heart attack, but maybe his bravado masked his fear. Whatever his reason, he'd volunteered to fill me in, and I intended to take him up on it.

"Nearly thirty years ago, I was a green patrol officer, just like your pal Dyson."

My frown when he referred to Mike Dyson, who was a nice young man, as my "pal" made him grin, and I knew he'd said it just to get a rise out of me.

"The first time I met the Durands, I was responding to a domestic incident call. They lived in a tiny apartment above the Corner Drugstore on First Street. Durand answered the door and told me everything was fine, but he'd been drinking and I couldn't see his wife, who'd made the call, so I insisted he let me in. I found her in the kitchen, crying. She said he'd slapped her. I asked her if she wanted to press charges, but she didn't. I figured I needed to get them separated until he sobered up, so I ended up taking him to his art teacher's house to spend the night."

"Ralph Anderson's house?"

"I don't remember the guy's name, but he lived all the way out on the end of Pine Street on a couple of acres. Nice ranch house and a big separate studio out back. He let Durand spend the night in the studio."

"That's Ralph's house. He still lives there."

The lieutenant shrugged. "Whatever. Same thing happened again a few weeks later, but Jill Durand still didn't want to press charges, so I took Durand back to his art teacher's place to spend the night. He told Durand he wasn't going to put up with any more of his drunken episodes, but he let him stay.

"The third time it happened, I arrested Durand, despite his wife's pleas not to, and he spent the night in jail. Of course, she bailed him out the next morning. I heard him sweet-talking her on their way out.

"Next thing I knew, we got a call that Jill Durand's missing up at Miner's Lookout. The chief organized a search party, and we searched for her from around noon until dark, without finding any trace of her. Durand was with us, but several people told us that he and his wife had gone off to a secluded spot to paint, and nobody had seen either one of them all morning.

"Well, I was sure he'd done something to her, even after he went home that night and told us that he found a note from her telling him she was leaving him. I figured he faked it, but the chief thought the note was legitimate because it was in her handwriting."

"For weeks afterward, I spent my time off searching for her body up by Miners' Lookout."

"You told me earlier that Jill really did leave Ulysses that day. When did you find out?"

"A few months later I ran into one of the art students who'd been at Miners' Lookout the day Jill disappeared, and she'd remembered that Jill had once mentioned that she had a friend who lived in Sedona. It wasn't much to go on, especially since she didn't know her name, but she told me she thought she worked in a restaurant over there."

"You found her, didn't you?"

"Sure did. A real stroke of luck. When I pulled into town, I stopped at a little restaurant for lunch, and there she was, waiting tables. When she saw me, she begged me not to tell Ulysses where she was. She said he was very possessive, but I let her know he'd left Lonesome Valley. Supposedly, he was headed to Mexico to get a divorce, but I had no way to confirm that. The chief had closed the missing person's case right after Durand found Jill's note, and when he found out I'd questioned Durand a couple of times after that, he read me the riot act."

"That's quite a story."

"Just goes to show you: not everything's a big mystery, Mrs. Trent," he said smugly.

I was about to tell him that there could still be a connection between Jill's disappearance years ago and Olivia's kidnapping when the nurse came in to give the lieutenant some medication, and I decided it was time for me to leave.

"Don't forget that cheeseburger," he called after me, eliciting a scowl from the nurse.

"Never going to happen," I replied.

Lieutenant Belmont wouldn't be an easy patient. His nurses had my sympathy.

Since I was already at the hospital, I decided to stop off on the second floor to check on Ulysses. The lieutenant's story about Ulysses's behavior years ago had cast him in a bad light, although he may have cleaned up his act in the meantime. Certainly Pamela hadn't mentioned that he'd been abusive toward her or struggled with a drinking problem. I hopped on the elevator and got off on the second floor, where I immediately spotted Brooks and Olivia conversing in the reception area.

"What are you doing here, Amanda?" Olivia asked. "I appreciate what you did, but there's no need to troll my husband."

"Excuse me," I said, putting the emphasis on "cuse." "Actually, I came to visit a friend on the fourth floor, who had a heart attack today, and it didn't seem right to leave without checking on Ulysses."

"Sorry, Amanda," Olivia muttered, as Brooks looked at her with raised eyebrows. "I'm afraid the stress is getting to me."

"We have some good news," Brooks told me. "Ulysses is showing signs that he's coming out of the coma. It's possible that he may wake up very soon."

"That *is* good news," I agreed. "I'm glad to hear it."

"I do appreciate your concern, Amanda," Olivia said. "It's been such a terrible week. I hope you can understand why I'm on edge, what with Ulysses's accident and the police investigation into the kidnapping. I had to answer questions from some local police detective for over an hour this morning. It was awful. He just kept asking me the same things over and over again until I thought I'd scream. If I never see that cop again, it'll be too soon!"

Chapter 21

I didn't tell Olivia that her chances of encountering Lieutenant Belmont again were slim, indeed, considering his poor health and the fact that the chief had assigned Sergeant Martinez to take over the case.

"Hang in there. It sounds as though things are looking up, at least," I told her.

"I'll go downstairs with you, Amanda," Brooks said, as I turned to leave. "I'm going to grab a drink while we're waiting for Gabrielle. Would you like me to bring you anything from the cafeteria, Olivia?"

"No, thanks. I'm fine." She picked up a home decorating magazine from the end table next to her and began paging through it. From the pace of her page turning, I could tell she was just passing time.

Brooks and I squeezed our way into the crowded elevator for the quick trip to the lobby. We stepped out, followed by the other visitors and the hospital personnel, and they went their separate ways.

"I'm going to drive Olivia back to the resort as soon as Gabrielle comes. Olivia wouldn't leave unless somebody is here for Ulysses." He glanced at his Rolex. "I don't know what's keeping her. She should have been here half an hour ago."

I hurriedly told Brooks goodbye after asking him to let me know how Ulysses was faring. I had no desire to see Gabrielle, not that she'd acknowledge my presence even if I did happen to run into her.

As I tooled up Canyon Drive on the way home, I saw Belle and Dennis walking with Laddie and Mr. Big parading in front of them. Belle had insisted on watching Laddie while I made my obligatory visit to the hospital. My canine companion had been more than happy to spend part of the evening with Mr. Big instead of Mona Lisa.

I pulled into my carport and went to greet them, stooping to pet our enthusiastic canines.

"You're a better person than I am," Dennis said. "When Belle told me you planned to visit Bill Beaumont in the hospital, I about fell off my chair."

"I can't take too much credit for that. If Dawn hadn't asked me to look in on him, it probably wouldn't have occurred to me."

"How is the grouchy curmudgeon?"

"Dawn told me his heart attack was serious, and he definitely does not look well. He's scheduled to have bypass surgery in a few days."

"Too bad. Even though I can't stand the guy, I wouldn't wish that on anyone."

We chatted for a few minutes until Laddie and I went inside to be greeted by Mona Lisa, who launched herself onto my shoulder, startling me. That was a new trick for her. I coaxed her into my arms for a cuddle, which she tolerated for a few seconds before leaping down and stalking off. She made herself scarce, while I unloaded the groceries I'd picked up on the way home and then tried to relax by watching a movie as Laddie curled up at my feet.

Mona Lisa reappeared the minute I went to bed, settling herself on her favorite pillow, next to me. I drifted off to sleep to the sound of her rhythmic purring and Laddie's soft breathing as he rested his chin on my feet.

The next morning proved uneventful, and I spent several hours painting in the studio after taking the time to snap some pictures of the Siamese cats' portrait to send to their proud pet parents. Luckily, I'd remembered to pick up batteries for the camera when I'd stopped at the store after visiting Lieutenant Belmont. Before pausing to have lunch, I emailed my invoice along with the pictures of the painting, hoping for a quick payment to bolster my checking account.

Since the regular Friday night studio tour was scheduled from six to nine, I spent some time tidying the studio, moving some paintings to different positions on the wall, and placing the two easels with my unfinished paintings in the center of the room to show them off to greater advantage. I had only three silk scarves available to display, and since I already had an order for half a dozen, I planned to dedicate some time tomorrow to dyeing several more. Even though each scarf sold for far less than a painting, scarf sales were profitable, and it took me much less time to dye a scarf than it did to create an original oil painting.

Laddie watched me as I bustled about the studio. He knew he'd be barred in the evening, but he'd become accustomed to the weekly gig and didn't mind watching the action from behind the baby gate that I always placed in the doorway between my studio and living room. Besides, Belle often came over on Friday nights to keep us company, although she didn't bring Mr. Big with her on these occasions because the little dog had a tendency to bark when he was excited. Laddie, on the other hand, always looked at the studio visitors with his usual friendly interest, and many of them stopped to pet him as he stuck his head over the baby gate.

I'd finished my task and was about to boot up my laptop to update my website when Brooks called with the news that Ulysses had been wide awake since early morning and was doing well. He'd made another request to see me so that he could thank me in person for delivering the ransom. It seemed so long ago since I'd gone to the hospital in response to his first request, only to learn that he'd fallen into a coma, but I realized it had been only a few days.

Ulysses remained something of an enigma, as far as I was concerned. Our acquaintance started in Brooks's new gallery during Ulysses's one-man show. After that, I'd observed him in action at the Roadrunner, the plein air paint-out, the auction, and finally in the magnificent resort suite Brooks had comped him while he'd stayed in Lonesome Valley. He'd been pleasant at the show and enjoyed seeing Ralph, although Ralph hadn't been quite as eager to renew their friendship. The same could be said of Pamela, who'd stepped back to avoid Ulysses's embrace when he'd stopped by the Roadrunner with Olivia. His remark to his wife had angered her, but it was difficult to tell how deeply because Susan had diplomatically spirited Olivia away at the time. I hadn't paid much attention to Ulysses at the paint-out because I'd needed to concentrate on my own artwork to finish on time, but he'd seemed genuinely distressed when he couldn't locate Olivia. He'd been frantic during the kidnapping affair, too. Both Pamela's and Lieutenant Belmont's accounts of Ulysses's behavior decades earlier suggested other, less-pleasant facets of his personality, although perhaps he had mellowed with time and left the binge drinking, abusive behavior, and cheating behind.

I fed Laddie and Mona Lisa an early dinner and then changed my clothes from the old jeans and t-shirt I'd been wearing to a fuchsia maxi dress. I draped one of my tie-dyed fuchsia and green scarves around my neck and put on some silver earrings with long, dangling chains. The last thing I did to get ready for the tour was yank another pesky gray hair from my hairline. I sighed, knowing that, at some point, there would be too many to pluck, and I'd have to decide whether to dye my hair back to its original dark brown shade or let it be a salt-and-pepper color.

It was nearly six o'clock, so I pulled my tour sign out to the curb and set it in place. I also turned on my new floodlights that Dennis had installed for me. If I didn't do it before darkness fell, I was likely to forget. Promptly at six, I put up the baby gate, but Laddie didn't protest since I'd remain in the living room with him until I spotted visitors arriving. I stationed myself on the sofa, where I could look out the front window and spot anybody who parked in front of my house or my neighbor's house.

Half an hour passed without anyone showing up, and it was beginning to look like it would be a very slow evening. I'd never had a tour end without any visitors, but that was always a possibility. I was about to call Belle to find out when she planned to join me, but as I reached for my phone, I saw a man approaching my sign on the curb. He paused to read the sign before walking toward my studio's door, so I stepped over the baby gate carefully, holding my long dress up so that I wouldn't trip. When my guest opened the door, I was ready to greet him, and so was Laddie, who crowded the baby gate and stuck his head over it so that he wouldn't miss anything.

"Hello," I beamed and launched into my standard elevator pitch, designed to be informative about my artwork without employing any high-pressure tactics, which I couldn't force myself to use, anyway. I always ended by inviting my visitors to look around and let me know if they had any questions.

"Umm. Very nice." He paused and looked uncertainly around. He looked as though he was about my age. He ran his hand through his short sandy hair and gave me a weak grin. "I saw your sign when I came out to trim my shrubs. I bought the house next door."

"Oh, you're our new neighbor." I introduced myself and Laddie.

He went to Laddie and petted him. "Nice dog."

"Laddie's a great companion. Do you have any pets?"

He stood by Laddie as though next to a lifeline. He hadn't even told me his name yet, so I didn't know what to call him.

"No. I'd like to, but I'm away on the job six months of the year, so it wouldn't be fair to have a pet I couldn't take care of half the time. I'm Brian, by the way, Brian Hudson."

"It's nice to meet you, Brian. Are you in sales, by any chance? My cousin's a sales rep, and he's away from home quite a bit, too."

"Oh, no, nothing like that. I work on an offshore oil rig in the Gulf of Mexico."

"Sounds dangerous."

"It can be, but most of the time, the job's fairly routine. Now that I'm a supervisor, I spend a lot of time on paperwork."

The door to the studio swung open, and Brian and I both turned to see who had come in.

"Belle, meet our new neighbor, Brian Hudson. Brian, Belle and her husband Dennis are my next-door neighbors on the other side."

Belle perked up immediately and joined Brian. Before we had a chance to continue our three-way conversation, several people entered the studio. Evidently, the family was vacationing in an RV, and Lonesome Valley was their first stop. They'd seen the ads for the Friday night studio tour, and they were stopping at each studio. For the next half hour, they kept me busy with their questions about my artwork. One of the women bought a couple of prints, and another one purchased a scarf.

When they left, I looked over at Laddie. Belle and Brian were attentively petting my affable retriever as they talked, and Laddie was enjoying every second of attention..

Belle gave me a thumbs-up. "Good sales!"

"Yes, not bad. Even if nobody else comes in this evening, it will have been worth it."

"Is your tour a weekly event?" Brian asked.

"Ten months out of the year. We take January and February off. There are twenty stops on the tour, but most people don't go to every one of them. I hope it won't disturb you. I know sometimes the visitors park in front of your house."

"No problem. Remember, I won't be home half the time, anyway, and when I am home, I'll probably be reading a book or watching TV. I can't imagine that it would bother me. Don't give it a second thought."

"I asked Brian to come over for a barbecue tomorrow night. You're coming, too, aren't you?" Belle grinned slyly.

This was the first time I'd heard of a Saturday night barbecue. She'd come up with it on the spur of the moment.

"Sure," I agreed, "and you have to let me contribute more than just dessert. I'll bring some potato salad and baked beans. Plus a pie."

"That's fine."

"I'm afraid I don't cook, but I'll be happy to bring some wine," Brian ventured.

"Good. Then it's all set," Belle said.

Brian had been looking around the studio while we talked. "I need something above my sofa in the living room," he said. "Do you have any prints about four feet wide?"

"Nothing that big on hand, but my art printer can make any size you need, so if you see a painting or a print you like, I can have one made for you in the right size, and it can be printed on art paper—I can show you samples—or on a canvas. With a gallery-wrap, you wouldn't need a frame."

"Lots of great choices, but I like that one best," he said, pointing to a colorful landscape that featured orange and green hues, "but I don't know if it would be the right color for my living room."

"Only one way to tell. I'll bring it over, and you can decide what you think, but it should be in the daytime. Natural light, you know."

"OK. Frankly, I'm not sure I'll know the difference, but you're an artist. You know all about colors, so I'll let you tell me whether it looks all right above my couch."

"I'd be happy to, but we want it to look better than all right. I'll give you my honest opinion. So will Belle."

I'd just volunteered Belle, but I knew she wouldn't mind. In fact, she'd be eager to satisfy her curiosity about our new neighbor and his house.

"Good. Is tomorrow OK? Maybe early afternoon?" he

suggested, and Belle and I agreed.

After Brian left, Belle and I stepped over the gate, into the living room, and I took up sentinel duty on the sofa. Content that no barrier separated us now, Laddie curled up at my feet.

Belle wiggled her eyebrows and gazed at me with a knowing look. "Don't you think he's kind of cute, Amanda?"

Chapter 22

"Who?"

"Very funny—Brian—that's who. You'll have the perfect opportunity to get to know him better tomorrow—two opportunities, actually. And I don't think I need to be with you when you take your painting over to his house."

"Please go with me, Belle. We'll need a second opinion, and you're great at interior decorating."

"Oh, all right. Why do I get the feeling you don't want to be alone with the man?"

"We don't really know him, and I don't want to jump into a romance with my next-door neighbor. It could prove to be very awkward."

"Or very pleasant."

"Let's just say I'm not in a big rush to have a man in my life. The last one left me for a woman my son's age."

"OK, I understand. You're not ready yet. It's probably better to take it slow and see how it goes. But just remember: Brian isn't Ned."

"I'll keep that in mind," I said with a smile. "Oh, here come a few people. I'd better go back into the studio."

"I'll stay here with Laddie. Good luck!" Belle called as I lifted up the skirt of my maxi-dress and climbed over the baby gate.

Minutes later, I rejoined Belle and Laddie.

"Tire kickers," I said. "I bet they're the last people we'll see this evening."

My prediction proved true. Nobody else visited my studio, so, promptly at nine, we wheeled the trolley out to the curb, hoisted my studio tour sign aboard, and pushed the cart back into the studio.

After I bade Belle goodnight, I thought about everything I had to do tomorrow, and I realized I might have overbooked. I put some dry beans in a pan to soak overnight and hauled out my crock pot from the cabinet under my kitchen counter. I'd debated whether or not to leave it behind in Kansas City when I'd moved to Lonesome Valley, but I was glad I'd brought it with me now. It would come in handy to cook the beans slowly all day without my having to constantly monitor them as I would have had to do if I'd used the oven instead.

Before I went to bed, I set my alarm. I had too much to do to allow myself the luxury of sleeping in, but when the alarm clock clanged at five-thirty, I reluctantly rolled out of bed.

After a walk to the park with Laddie, I drained the softened beans and dumped them into my crock pot along with water, molasses, brown sugar, a chopped onion, bacon, ketchup, mustard, and some salt and pepper. I was about ready to turn on my crock pot when I thought better of it. Mona Lisa had a bad habit of leaping onto the kitchen counter when I least expected it. Since I wouldn't be home to keep an eye on her all day, I moved the crock pot to the patio and plugged it in there. Even though chances were that she'd ignore it, I thought it was better to be safe than sorry.

I scrubbed some potatoes and quickly assembled a peach pie,

glad I'd had the foresight a few weeks ago to make pastry and freeze a dozen pie crusts. I squeezed the potatoes and peach pie into the oven and set my timer for an hour.

While the pie and potatoes baked, I showered and dressed for my trip to the hospital to see Ulysses. I planned on making my visit with him short. With luck, I'd be back home in an hour, so I'd have time to dye some scarves before my one-o'clock appointment with my new neighbor.

I really couldn't delay the dyeing until tomorrow if I wanted to deliver the half-dozen scarves to the hospital gift shop on Monday morning, as I'd promised Xena.

After I dyed them and they were dry, I needed to steam each scarf separately to set the dye, and that took some time.

As soon as the timer went off, I removed the baked potatoes and pie from the oven and set them in my tiny pantry, away from my curious pets, to cool. Then I assured Laddie I would be back soon and departed. Although Mona Lisa wasn't around when I left, I was glad I'd secured the food for the barbecue out of her reach.

This time, I didn't even bother trying to find a spot in the hospital's small lot. I parked a couple of blocks away and walked. I was in for a surprise when a couple of police cars whizzed by me and turned into the hospital's emergency entrance.

Perhaps they were investigating an auto accident, I speculated, but I hadn't seen an ambulance, and the only sirens I'd heard had been those of the police cruisers.

I saw no activity in the lobby when I entered, and I assumed that whatever had brought the police to the hospital was happening in the emergency room.

Figuring that Ulysses wouldn't stay in the ICU since Brooks

had told me he was not only awake but was also feeling well, I stopped to ask the receptionist his room number and was directed to the fourth floor. By the number, I knew Ulysses's room was just a few doors down from Lieutenant Belmont's. Nevertheless, I planned to avoid the lieutenant on this visit, which I resolved to keep short. I really didn't want to get into another discussion about his diet.

As soon as I got off the elevator, I knew something was wrong. Several patrol officers were huddled around the nursing station, opposite the elevator. I headed down the same hallway I'd used the previous day, but I didn't get far before one of them came after me.

"Ma'am, unless you're a hospital staffer, I'm going to have to ask you to leave."

"But why? What's going on?"

"Please just do as I ask."

I glanced toward the end of the hallway and spotted Mike Dyson. I waved at him, hoping he'd notice me. Luckily, I'd caught his eye, and he came over.

"Mike, what's going on?"

"I tried to tell her she needs to leave," the officer who'd warned me told Mike.

"It's OK, Jake. I know this lady."

With a shrug, Jake returned to the nursing station.

"What's going on, Mike?" I repeated. "Why are you here?"

"Ulysses Durand's dead. He's been strangled."

Chapter 23

I put my hand over my mouth and stood there, frozen, staring at Mike. I couldn't believe it. To have recovered from a life-threatening accident and pulled out of a coma, only to have his life snuffed out by a killer—it was unbelievable.

"I'm sorry, Amanda."

"I'm shocked. How could this happen? He should have been safe in the hospital." Even as I said it, though, I could imagine that it wouldn't have been too difficult to avoid detection in the busy hospital, especially since the employees and patients would have no reason to suspect a bad actor. Employees and visitors were there to help patients, not harm them.

"Say, were you coming to visit Ulysses? Is that why you're here?"

I nodded.

"In that case, you'd better wait a minute. The chief or Sergeant Martinez might want to talk to you."

"All right, but I don't know what I could tell them. I just arrived a few minutes ago."

Mike disappeared into Ulysses's room and returned with Sergeant Martinez. I explained the reason for my visit, and he told me that I could go home, but that he might need to speak with me again later. He leaned over and spoke quietly so that I was the only one who could hear him, and he explained that he thought Ulysses's murder might be related to his wife's kidnapping. I could understand his point; two crimes targeting the same couple within a week didn't exactly seem coincidental.

"Of course. I don't know what I could add, but let me know if you need me." I looked past Sergeant Martinez to see Lieutenant Belmont emerge from his room, dressed in a blue hospital gown and pulling a metal IV stand along beside him.

"I thought I heard you, Dave," he said. "What's all the commotion?"

"Durand's dead," Sergeant Martinez said bluntly.

"Didn't come out of the coma, huh?"

"Oh, he did. Somebody strangled him right there in his room."

"Better let me have a look," Lieutenant Belmont said.

"Oh, no, you don't. You're a patient, remember? The chief's here, too. We'll take care of the investigation. You'd better get back to bed before your nurse shows up."

"She made me walk all around the floor this morning. I don't think she'll mind."

"Baloney. You had a heart attack yesterday, man. You're supposed to be on sick leave."

"But I can help. I'm the only real detective you've got."

"Go back to your room, Bill. I'm not kidding. I have work to do here. I'll stop by later and fill you in."

The lieutenant didn't look happy. "OK, but I need help." He looked at me speculatively. "She'll do. Push this contraption back in there for me, will you, Mrs. Trent?"

Despite being pretty sure that the lieutenant's request for my help amounted to nothing more than a ruse, I did as he asked. As soon as he settled himself back in bed, I learned the real reason he'd turned to me.

"You're tight with Dave and Mike," he said. "I want to know everything that's happening with the Durand investigation."

"Why ask me? Sergeant Martinez already told you he'd keep you informed."

"Dawn won't go for that. She thinks I need rest and no stress. There's no way she'll let him tell me a thing. The chief and Dave—they're good cops, but they're not detectives."

If he hadn't been so down and out, I might have been tempted to remind him that he hadn't done such a bang-up job of solving the last murder in Lonesome Valley, but, as matters stood, I thought it best not to say anything that would agitate him further.

We were interrupted by a hospital technician who had come to draw blood, and I slipped out of the lieutenant's room without making him any promises.

The hallway was so crowded by the time I left the lieutenant's room that, still trying to wrap my brain around the fact that Ulysses had been murdered in his own hospital room, I decided to take the stairs, just a few feet away at the end of the hall. I'd gone down a flight when I heard the sound of a door closing. Someone on one of the floors above had entered the stairwell.

I stopped. Instinctively, I looked up, behind me and shuddered as a chill went through me. Taking the stairs instead of the elevator had seemed like a good idea. The hallway on the fourth floor, where I'd visited Ulysses, was busy. The stairs weren't used much, especially by visitors, so I'd thought I could avoid the crowded hallway and elevator and hasten my departure.

But, now, I was alone.

I was vulnerable.

I heard nothing more.

Looking up, all I could see from my present vantage point was the flight of stairs I'd just descended and the railing along the stairs' edge. I didn't see anyone. No shadows loomed or shifted on the stairs, either.

Whoever I'd heard had decided not to take the stairs, after all, I told myself. I exhaled. I hadn't even realized that I'd been holding my breath. I felt tense and stressed.

There's no reason to be frightened, I told myself, as I started down the stairs. Then I remembered that Brooks originally hadn't wanted to report Olivia's kidnapping to the police because he'd feared that the kidnappers could retaliate. He'd thought I might be in danger, too.

Footsteps! On the stairs above me!

I froze.

There was no mistaking the sounds.

Someone was on the stairs, after all.

And I was alone.

I'd been foolish to take the stairs, putting myself in jeopardy. Ulysses had been murdered, and his killer was on the loose. The murderer could still be in the hospital. Maybe whoever the killer was had entered the stairwell to pursue *me*.

Listening intently, I hurriedly descended the stairs.

Sure enough, the footsteps continued, echoing hollowly in the high space of the stairwell. When my pace increased, so did theirs. I didn't know where my stalker had entered the stairwell or how far above me the person might be.

I paused, glancing up, but the levels of the staircase doubled back on themselves at the landings connecting the sections of stairs, forming a rectangle, and the structure impeded my vision.

I knew one thing, though. If Ulysses's killer had decided I, too, must die, he was more than capable of achieving his goal. Whoever had strangled Ulysses had murdered him right in the middle of a busy hospital. My only hope was to get down the stairs before my stalker caught up to me.

Except for my own labored breathing, I heard nothing.

The footsteps had stopped.

Had my pursuer paused, too, to listen?

Above me, I heard a door close.

Then silence.

Ready to resume my flight at a moment's notice, I waited, listening.

A minute passed; I heard nothing.

I continued down the stairs without incident.

Whoever had entered the stairwell above me had obviously exited.

Had I been targeted by Ulysses's killer, or was the presence of another person on the stairwell due to nothing more sinister than a visitor who, like me, had merely found the stairs more convenient than the elevator?

Perhaps I'd never know. Perhaps I was letting my imagination run away with me.

But I did know one thing. I was alone again.

Chapter 24

My heart still racing, I hastened down the remaining stairs. The bright lights, the sight of the people in the lobby, and the receptionist at the desk near the front entrance were a welcome relief, indeed!

As I crossed the lobby, I saw Olivia, Gabrielle, and Brooks rushing into the main entrance. Now didn't seem the best time to offer condolences, so I stepped around a corner, out of sight, until they'd boarded the elevator.

The shock of learning about Ulysses's untimely demise stayed with me as I drove home with the sickening feeling that if the police had known about the kidnapping earlier, perhaps Ulysses would still be alive. On the other hand, I could be wrong, and the two crimes could be unrelated.

Busy as the hospital was, anybody could go into a patient's room unnoticed. Whoever the murderer was must be a strong person. Both Mike and Sergeant Martinez had said Ulysses had been strangled. I couldn't imagine how anybody could do that to another person; it was terrible to contemplate.

I wondered whether I should call Pamela to let her know has died. I didn't really want to be the bearer of bad tidings, but I also didn't want her to hear about it on the news.

I decided to make a detour by the gallery so that I could talk to her. When I arrived, I had to park in the town's downtown lot because there wasn't an empty parking space on Main Street. As I walked toward the gallery, a bus pulled up out front, and a crowd of tourists streamed off the vehicle and into the gallery. With so many people around, it was going to be difficult to grab a minute alone with Pamela. I was on the verge of turning around when I saw Valerie, one of our members who taught art at the high school, frantically gesturing to me to come inside. I couldn't very well ignore her.

"Hi, Valerie. I stopped by to see Pamela. What's up?"

"I'm here all alone. Pamela hasn't shown up yet, and Frank called to say he'd be delayed, something about having to take his son to an emergency dental visit. Can you help out for a while?"

"OK, sure," I said, hoping that Frank or Pamela would show up soon. I still had scarves to dye, potato salad to prepare, and a call on my next-door neighbor to make so that we could see how the painting he liked would look in his living room. I started to panic, but there was no time to think about all the tasks that I'd planned when the immediate one was right in front of me.

A few of the tourists had gathered at the jewelry counter, and I went to assist them while Valerie answered questions about the paintings on display.

Soon she was removing one from the wall and ringing up a sale for it. Rather than lugging a bulky painting around downtown for several hours, the couple who'd purchased it requested that we hold it for them to pick up before their bus departed in the afternoon. This was a common practice, and Valerie readily agreed.

By the time the crowd thinned, I'd sold several pieces of jewelry, and Valerie had sold some packets of note cards and a few prints. The rush over, we looked at each other, and she gave me a thumbs-up.

"Thanks for staying to help, Amanda. I can't imagine why Pamela isn't here yet. She's usually the first to arrive."

I glanced outside and saw a big SUV double park in front of the gallery. Pamela got out and waved to the driver. The windows were tinted so dark that I couldn't see who it was, but I assumed Rich was the one who'd dropped her off.

"Good morning, ladies," Pamela said breezily when she came in. "How's it going?"

I could tell Valerie was irritated as she explained that she'd pressed me into action because she'd been the only member who'd shown up to work.

Pamela didn't catch on, although normally she would have been concerned about any glitch that might interfere with the smooth operations of the gallery. Instead, she smiled and murmured "uh huh," then went down the hallway to her office. In a few seconds, we could hear her singing, although she stopped after a few bars.

Valerie shook her head. "I think I'll call Frank to find out if he's going to show up. If not, maybe Dorothy or Dawn might be able to take his place; that is, unless you can stay."

"I'd rather not. It's just that I have a ton of things I need to do this afternoon." I explained about my scarf orders and the in-house showing of my painting.

"OK. I'm sure I can find someone to come in. Why don't you head on home? I'll call Pamela out of her office to help if it gets busy again."

"I need to talk to Pamela for a minute first. That's why I

stopped by. It's bad news, I'm afraid." I told Valerie about Ulysses.

"Murdered? He seemed like such a nice man. I mean I only saw him a couple of times, but I can't believe somebody would want to kill him."

"Pamela knew him better than the rest of us, so I thought I should tell her before she hears it elsewhere."

I wasn't looking forward to giving her the news, especially when she was in such a good mood, but I thought I should.

She looked up from tapping her computer keyboard, as I walked into her office.

"I'm putting the finishing touches on our newsletter." She clicked the mouse.

"Pamela, I'm afraid I have some bad news."

My statement seemed to get through to her, and her mood turned serious immediately.

"What is it?"

"Ulysses is dead."

"Oh, no! He never came out of the coma," she moaned.

"It's actually worse than that."

She stared at me. "What could be worse?"

"He was murdered, strangled right in his hospital bed."

"That can't be! How could this happen? Oh, poor Ulysses!" Pamela started to cry, and, before I knew it, she was sobbing.

"I'm so sorry, Pamela," I said, feeling guilty at having upset her. She grabbed a wad of tissues from the box on her desk, and now it was empty. I ran to the restroom to find another box to replace the empty one. I located some supplies in the bathroom cabinet, grabbed a new box of tissues, tore it open, and returned to Pamela's office. I offered her the box, and she grabbed a handful of tissues.

"Thanks, Amanda," she sniffed.

I was glad to see she had calmed down a little bit. "Would you like a glass of water?" I asked.

The door opened before she had a chance to answer me, and there was Rich, a bag from the bakery down the block in his hand. He set it on Pamela's desktop and went around her desk to embrace her.

"What's wrong, honey?"

"Ulysses has been murdered!"

"The artist?"

"Yes. You know, the one who set up the plein air paint-out and auction."

"Well, that's a shame, but you hardly knew the guy. Why are you so upset?"

I took his question as my cue to tiptoe out of the office. I had a feeling that Pamela's long-past relationship with Ulysses was about to become an issue just when they had evidently reconciled their differences over Chip's presence in the gallery. I didn't look back after I gently closed Pamela's office door, but by the time I reached the end of the hallway, I could hear their raised voices.

"Trouble in paradise?" Valerie asked.

"I guess so."

"It's too bad. Pamela was in such a good mood when she came in."

I wished Rich hadn't come in when he had. If only Pamela had had a chance to pull herself together, the whole situation could have been avoided. She'd told me his jealousy had kicked in lately, and I'd witnessed it myself when he'd insisted she resign as gallery director. I didn't know how jealous he could be of a dead man, but I believed he didn't want Pamela to have feelings for any man except him.

I pulled my cell phone out of my pocket and was dismayed to see that the time had really gotten away from me. Belle and I were due at our new neighbor's in a few minutes. Rather than rushing through our visit with him, I decided to postpone it. I still had scarves to dye before the barbecue, and I needed to get started.

I called Belle, explained the situation, and asked her to let Brian know.

"Don't worry, Amanda. I'll take care of it. Shall I try to reschedule for the same time tomorrow afternoon?"

"Perfect. I hope he's not angry."

"He struck me as a level-headed guy. I'm sure he'll understand that you have work to do, and you couldn't very well leave Valerie in the lurch at the gallery."

"I hope so."

"Leave it to me. I'll see you at six. I don't know what the world's coming to—another murder in Lonesome Valley!"

"Yes. It's awful. I was so shocked when Mike told me."

We didn't linger on the phone. I knew Belle would have to visit Brian in person to ask to delay our appointment because neither of us had his phone number. I hated to postpone, but I knew I'd never finish everything else I had to do if I kept the appointment.

Once home, I slapped together a sandwich for lunch, gave Laddie and Mona Lisa a snack, and rushed to peel the potatoes I'd boiled earlier. After I cut them into chunks, I chopped an onion and made the potato salad for the barbecue. I put it into the refrigerator to chill. Finally, I was ready to dye a dozen silk scarves.

Dyeing was a messy process, so I always used vinyl gloves to protect my hands and did all my dyeing outside. I planned to tie-dye most of the scarves and use a watercolor-effect technique with a salt resist on the rest.

Using wide rubber bands, I tied the scarves individually after folding them to produce different effects. Laddie ran around the yard while I worked at the picnic table. Soon, he came over with his ball in his mouth, wanting to play fetch. I took a few minutes to oblige him before returning to the scarves. I prepared dye in plastic squirt bottles so that I could apply it easily. After I finished the tie-dyed scarves, I moved on to the watercolor style, which involved tacking the scarf to a wooden frame before applying the dye and salt. I had only one frame, so I was forced to dye each of these one at a time. I had to let each scarf dry before removing it from the frame and starting another one. Luckily, the low Arizona humidity ensured they'd dry quickly.

I barely had time to shower and dress for the barbecue, but at least all I had to do the next day was steam and press the scarves. I slipped Laddie's leash around my arm and grabbed the bowl of potato salad. I planned to drop him off and come back for the beans and the pie, but as soon as Belle saw us coming, she called Dennis, who took the bowl and Laddie so that Belle and I could collect the rest of the food from my house.

Dennis was in the backyard with Laddie and Mr. Big, and Belle was preparing a green salad when Brian rang the doorbell. Since they were busy, I answered the door and invited Brian in, apologizing profusely for postponing the showing of my landscape in his living room.

"No problem," he said. "We can do it another time."

Maybe it was my imagination, but I sensed he was less than

pleased by what I'd done. I led him to the kitchen, where he handed Belle a large bottle of wine. She, in turn, took him out to the patio and introduced him to Dennis, and the two seemed to hit it off right away.

Belle and I withdrew to the kitchen.

"I get the feeling Brian's a little put out with me," I told her.

"Really? He seemed fine when I asked him if we could bring the painting over tomorrow."

"So we do have an appointment for tomorrow?"

She nodded.

"Maybe I misunderstood him."

"I think he might feel a little bit shy and awkward around you."

"Me? Why?"

"Because he's attracted to you."

"You really think so? I sure didn't get that impression."

"Mark my words."

Chapter 25

Frankly, I thought Brian's supposed attraction to me was a figment of Belle's imagination. Although he acted polite toward me during dinner, he seemed more enthusiastic about the food than me, not that I cared one way or the other. Romance didn't figure in my plans for the near future and perhaps not for the far future, either.

After dinner, I helped Belle clear and put away the dishes, despite her urging me to stay outside, where Dennis and Brian were playing tug-of-war with the dogs.

When it came time to leave, I told Belle I'd pick up my serving dishes the next day, but she insisted that Brian could help me carry them home. He could hardly refuse his hostess's request, so he awkwardly agreed. He didn't say a word to me as we walked the short distance to my kitchen door and I unlocked it.

I'd left lights on in the carport and the kitchen. I let Laddie run inside, ahead of me, and, as I turned to take the large bowls from Brian, he bumped into me but managed not to drop the bowls.

I don't think I've ever seen anybody look so embarrassed.

"I'm sorry. I'm such a klutz," he apologized, turning red.

"Not at all. It was my fault," I replied, trying to set him at ease. I was beginning to think Belle had accurately pegged him as somewhat shy.

He followed me inside and put the bowls on the kitchen counter, but he didn't look at me when I thanked him. He was out the door, still staring at his shoes, when I called after him.

"See you tomorrow."

Finally, he looked at me, this time like a deer in the headlights.

"Tomorrow?"

"Yes, Belle and I will bring the painting you liked over, so you can see if it would look good in your living room."

"Oh, right! OK," he mumbled, walking away with an ungainly wave.

I closed the door, locked it, and stooped to unsnap Laddie's leash. I was glad he'd enjoyed a lot of play time during the evening, but now he was a tired dog. Mona Lisa, on the other hand, ran around in a kitty frenzy until I took out her favorite feather toy, flicking it back and forth while she tried to pounce on it.

While I played with Mona Lisa, I remembered that, when the topic of Ulysses's murder had come up during dinner, Dennis and Belle had both steered the conversation in another direction, probably not wanting to dwell on crime in Lonesome Valley, since Brian had mentioned that one of the reasons he'd decided to relocate here was that Lonesome Valley seemed like a nice small town.

Ulysses had certainly been a target; his murder hadn't been caused by a random attack, and I definitely didn't think the citizens of Lonesome Valley were in any danger from the killer, who had some reason for wanting the famous artist dead. I wondered what the motive could be—revenge, love, money?

No obvious answer came to mind. I didn't envy Sergeant Martinez's task in investigating the crime. As far as I could tell, there were no cameras in the hospital rooms or hallways. I hadn't seen any in the stairwell, either. The perpetrator could have easily walked in and out of the hospital without anyone noticing, but if the police had videos of the fourth-floor hallway, they would be able to review them to find out who'd entered Ulysses's room, but without them, there was no way to tell. I wondered if they'd found any evidence in his room; if so, I doubted that they would share it.

With a yawn, I realized how tired I felt, so I headed to bed, not bothering to set the alarm clock. I could count on Laddie to wake me up at six since the piercing buzzing of the alarm clock wouldn't awaken us earlier.

Sure enough, promptly at six, I felt a wet nose nudging my arm. My canine companion wagged his tail happily, as I rolled out of bed and gave him a hug. Mona Lisa gazed at us. Turning her back, she curled up on her favorite pillow and stayed in bed.

Laddie and I took a leisurely walk in the park and returned home to an equally leisurely breakfast. I didn't feel as rushed as I had the day before. By the time I had a pot of strong tea, I was ready to get to work, but I remembered that I hadn't heard back yet from the couple who'd commissioned the portrait of the Siamese cats. I went into the studio and booted up my laptop, since I reserved it for business and used my phone for personal email.

Still, no response. I thought it unusual that I hadn't received any messages from them, nor had they paid the invoice I'd sent them. I decided to give it the rest of the day, and if I still hadn't heard from them, I'd contact them by phone in the morning. They'd always answered my previous emails promptly, and I began to fear that they hadn't liked the portrait and were delaying telling me. I hoped that wasn't the case, especially since I was counting on their final payment arriving soon. At least, I'd have Xena's check for the scarves tomorrow, but that alone wouldn't be enough to see me through.

Perhaps my neighbor would buy a print of the painting he liked. I should probably pitch some more boutiques and gift shops to purchase my scarves, too.

Thinking about my finances wasn't helping me get any work done, though, and I couldn't deliver any scarves to the hospital gift shop if I didn't finish preparing them.

It was important to steam set the dye on my silk scarves to make them colorfast and washable. They could be dry cleaned, too, as long as the dye was set properly, so it was an important step in finishing the scarves. Long ago, I'd decided the microwave steaming method was the way to go, especially since a professional steaming device cost well over a thousand dollars. I'd bought a second microwave for that very purpose. I stored it in the carport on a rolling cart, so I could move it easily to work on the patio.

It was time to get to work now, so I pushed the cart to the patio, plugged the microwave into an exterior outlet, and began wrapping each scarf in paper. It would take just a few minutes in the microwave with a cup of water to steam set each scarf, but they had to be done individually, rather than all together.

The morning flew, and I felt I'd accomplished a lot. After pressing all dozen scarves, I set aside six to take to the gift shop in the morning and printed an invoice to drop off at the same time for Xena's records.

Soon it was time to get ready for the showing. I shed my jeans and t-shirt and put on some tan cotton pants, which didn't wrinkle as badly as my linen slacks and a royal blue tunic top with an asymmetrical hem. I was looking for my paper samples when Belle came to the door, and my phone rang at the same time. She slipped inside while I looked at the display to see who was calling. It was Dawn Martinez, so I answered the call while Belle greeted Laddie and Mona Lisa showed up to rub against her ankles.

"Hi, Dawn."

"Amanda, it's Dave. I borrowed Dawn's phone. I was wondering if you could come into the station this afternoon. I'm conducting interviews, but it shouldn't take long. Say two o'clock?"

"I don't think I can come in then, Sergeant. I'm on my way out to show a painting in a customer's home."

"We can make it later this afternoon, if that works for you. I'd really like to wrap up the preliminary interviews today."

"All right. I can probably be there sometime between three and four."

"Police?" Belle asked after I put my phone down. "I heard you say 'Sergeant.'"

I nodded. "Yes, that was Dawn's husband, Sergeant Martinez. He wants to ask me a few questions about Olivia's kidnapping. They don't know whether it's related to Ulysses's murder or not."

"I'm glad you didn't have to cancel again. I think Brian's serious about wanting to buy a print."

"Let me find my paper samples." I rummaged through my desk and located them tucked inside a cardboard sleeve.

"Do you need help carrying the painting?"

"No. I can get it if you'll take the paper samples."

Brian must have been looking for us because he opened the

door before we started up his front sidewalk. When he ushered us into his living room, I could see that he wasn't kidding about needing a painting to hang above his sofa. The living room walls, painted a neutral eggshell hue, were completely bare, and the earth-tone furniture all looked new. There weren't any decorative knick-knacks in evidence, although a few magazines and a book lay on the coffee table.

"It's hung on a wire, isn't it?" he asked, and when I answered him in the affirmative, he continued. "Good. I've installed a sturdy hook in the stud centered above the sofa. Shall we?"

He hoisted the painting up, securing the wire on the hook and stood back to determine whether the position needed to be fine-tuned.

"A little bit up on the left," I suggested, and Brian nudged the canvas.

"That looks perfect now," Belle commented. "It certainly brightens up the room. You could pick up some of the colors in the painting with pillows and other accent pieces, maybe a couple of vases."

Brian scratched his head and flashed a lopsided grin. He looked at me for confirmation.

"I agree with Belle, but, of course, I'm biased since I painted it. What do *you* think?"

"I really like it and Belle's suggestions, too."

"Great! We brought some paper samples." Belle handed me the cardboard sleeve, and I took the samples out and fanned them, much like a pack of cards. "See: each one is a little different. You can feel the surface textures." I handed most of them to Brian. "Those are all archival art papers. Here are three more, but these are different types of canvas."

Brian studied the samples. "They're all nice, but I like the original painting best. I think I'll go with that. What are the damages?" he asked, pulling a check and a pen out of his pocket.

I gasped. "Are you sure? The prints are a lot less expensive."

"I'm sure."

"The original is four thousand dollars."

"OK," Brian said without hesitation. He wrote the check and handed it to me.

"Anything wrong?"

I must have looked taken aback. "It's just that every time I sell a painting, I realize I can't afford to buy my own work."

Brian burst out laughing.

Belle shook her head at my uncensored reaction.

"Thank you so much," I stammered. "I really appreciate it." Now who was acting flustered? I could have kicked myself. Sales skills had never been my strong suit, but I managed to muddle through, knowing that creating artwork would always be easier for me than selling it.

"Brian seemed a lot more relaxed in his own home," Belle said, as we walked back to my house.

"I noticed. I still can't believe he bought the painting and not a print. It was so pricey."

"I'm sure he can afford it. Dennis told me he'd been living in a small apartment in Phoenix for years before finally deciding to buy a house, and his job pays well. I wouldn't worry about it. He wouldn't have bought the original if he didn't want it."

"It seemed impulsive, but I do think the painting makes a great focal point for his living room."

"Yes, it does, so stop worrying about it. If his check bounces, we can always show up on his doorstep and repossess it."

"You don't think—" I had a sudden moment of panic.

"I'm kidding, Amanda. I'm sure everything will be fine."

As I drove to the police station later, I was still thinking in amazement about my unexpected high-dollar sale, which had immediately eased the pressure I'd felt over this month's finances. I still intended to follow up on the Siamese cats' pet portrait, but it was less urgent to collect my final payment for it now.

When I arrived at the station, I found Mike behind the desk, rather than Sergeant Martinez.

"Oh, hi, Amanda. Dave will be with you soon. He's finishing up an interview now, but it shouldn't be long. Have a seat."

I did as he requested, sitting in one of the garish orange plastic chairs in the LVPD's reception area. I pulled my phone from my purse and idly began checking my messages, but there was nothing of consequence. I looked up when the door opened. Brooks came in, saw me, and pulled up a chair.

"I stepped out for a minute. I've already been interviewed, and Gabrielle's back there now, but she doesn't know anything, so it shouldn't take long."

"How's Olivia holding up?" I asked.

"About as well as can be expected, I suppose. I feel terrible about everything. If they hadn't come here for the show, Olivia wouldn't have been kidnapped and Ulysses might still be alive. I've offered Olivia the use of the suite at the resort for as long as she needs it."

"You can't blame yourself, Brooks. For all we know, the kidnappers and murderer followed them here. Maybe they thought it would be easier to get away with crime in a small town."

"I suppose that's true, but I can't help feeling guilty. As if that weren't enough, an art critic in Los Angeles wrote a blog post implying that I might have had something to do with Ulysses's death since the prices of his artwork will be going up now that he's not around to produce any more paintings."

"Really? That's awful."

"He's right about one thing. The prices will be going up. This morning, I checked his work at three galleries, and they've all raised the prices for Ulysses's paintings. I'd be neglecting my fiduciary responsibility as a gallery owner not to do the same."

When I didn't respond, he said, "Amanda, surely you don't think I had anything to do with Ulysses's death. He was my friend."

"No. Of course not, It's just a little mind-blowing that the galleries have raised prices so fast."

"Standard business practice—it's a matter of supply and demand."

We heard the staccato click-click of high heels on the tile floor, and Gabrielle came into the reception area, followed by Sergeant Martinez. As usual, she ignored me completely. Brooks jumped to his feet and followed her out the door without another word. Sergeant Martinez watched as the couple left the building.

"He has his hands full being married to that one," he said. "She acts like she's the queen bee. Come on back, Amanda. Would you like a cup of coffee or a soda?"

"No, thanks, Sergeant."

"You don't need to keep calling me sergeant. It's Dave."

"OK, Dave." It felt a bit odd to call him by his first name, but since he'd asked me to, I complied.

Dave turned out to be a methodical questioner as he asked me to relate what I knew about the kidnapping and how I'd delivered the ransom. Then, he turned to Ulysses's stay in the hospital, but I really couldn't enlighten him about any of the events that had happened there. Although Ulysses had asked me to visit him twice, I'd never actually seen him during his hospital stay.

"That about wraps it up, Amanda. Just one more question. Do you happen to know anyone by the name of Jill?"

"Not personally, but I have heard of a Jill."

"Go on."

"Jill Durand was Ulysses's first wife. She left him during a plein air paint-out at Miners' Lookout twenty-eight years ago."

"Do you know whether Ulysses was still in touch with her?"

"Not that I'm aware, but I really have no idea. Olivia would probably know."

"I'll check with her. The name didn't come up until I talked to Brooks Miller a little while ago. He said that when Ulysses first came out of his coma, he insisted that he'd seen Jill, and he wanted Brooks to go find her so he could see her again."

"Do you think she could be the murderer?"

"Stranger things have happened, but I suspect Durand was just confused. Could be he saw someone who looked like her or maybe he imagined it."

"You might want to check with Lieutenant Belmont. He knew Jill back in the day."

"He told you that?"

I nodded.

"Well, I'll be. Thanks for the tip, but I'd better not say anything that'll agitate him at the moment, even though Dawn and I plan on visiting him this evening. They've moved his surgery up. Now it's scheduled for tomorrow morning."

Chapter 26

I timed my arrival at the hospital's gift shop for a few minutes after opening. I didn't recognize either of the women on duty, but evidently they had been expecting me because they recognized my name as soon as I told them who I was. I exchanged my scarves for the check Xena had left for me, marked the invoice I'd prepared "paid," and handed it to one of the women. When I left, they were busy arranging the new scarves on the rack Dennis had built.

As I tucked the check into my wallet next to the check Brian had given me, I thought about how nice it would be not to have to hustle for the small sales, but I was grateful for any sale I could make at this stage in my career as an emerging artist. I realized that it was unlikely I'd ever achieve the acclaim that Ulysses had, but I was happy being able to make a living from my artwork, although sometimes it did seem like a struggle.

My next stop was the bank, but since I was already at the hospital, I thought I should check on Lieutenant Belmont. He'd probably be in surgery right now, but maybe one of the nurses could give me an update.

I took the elevator to the fourth floor and went to his room at the end of the hallway. I'd expected it to be empty, but there he was, sitting up in bed with a scowl on his face.

He perked up when he saw me.

"Mrs. Trent, could you please get me a glass of water?"

I started to do as he'd asked, but there was no water in the pitcher or cup on his tray.

"Wait a minute. You're not supposed to be drinking anything before surgery."

He crossed his arms and muttered something I couldn't hear. It probably wasn't anything I wanted to hear, anyway, but a doctor came into the room before I had a chance to ask him to repeat himself.

A tall woman who towered over me introduced herself as the anesthesiologist. She explained what she'd be doing and asked the lieutenant to confirm that he hadn't eaten or drunk anything since midnight.

"How could I?" he groused. "They don't even feed me anything edible when they do let me eat."

"So I take it that's a 'no,'" she said.

The lieutenant grunted his response.

"I see you haven't had any previous surgeries. Is that correct?"

"Yup."

After a few more questions, which the lieutenant answered with the same monosyllabic responses, she said that she'd see him soon and assured him that she'd monitor him closely.

"Could I see you for a moment?" she asked with a bob of her head, indicating that I should join her in the hall.

"I'm afraid your husband isn't taking his condition very seriously. He's going to need to follow doctor's orders if he wants to recover."

"He's not my husband," I whispered. She hadn't been talking very quietly, and I thought the lieutenant had probably heard her, despite the fact that we'd left his room.

"Oh, I'm sorry. I just assumed."

"Let's move away from the door," I urged, as I took a few steps. "I think he's scared," I told her in a quiet voice, "but he'd never admit it."

"I see. Well, we have a good record of success with this type of surgery, as I'm sure his surgeon has told him, but it helps a lot if the patient cooperates."

"I understand." I doubted that the lieutenant would stick to any regimen that included a cardiac diet and exercise, but I could be wrong. Maybe he'd turn over a new leaf.

"If you have any influence on him, maybe you could get him to see the light."

I nodded, but I knew that nothing that I or anyone else could say would make a bit of difference. The lieutenant would do exactly as he pleased.

When the doctor hurried off, I stood there for a few seconds, debating with myself whether or not to return to the lieutenant's room.

"Mrs. Trent," he bellowed.

"Stop that yelling!" I said, returning to his room. "There are other patients around here, you know."

"Yeah, yeah."

A male nurse came in and told Lieutenant Belmont they would be moving him, to prep him for surgery. I noticed that the lieutenant didn't have any smart remarks to offer the man, but when another nurse, a young woman, came in, he said, "Nurse Ratched, I presume."

She ignored him. I guessed she'd had to deal with plenty of difficult patients, and perhaps ignoring some of their absurd statements was one way to handle them.

Lieutenant Belmont looked at her to see if he'd provoked a reaction, but his expression quickly changed when she came closer.

"*Jill?*"

She pointed to her name tag, which was pinned to her scrubs. "No, it's Samantha. My name's Samantha."

"Oh." He lay back and closed his eyes, as though he'd finally reconciled himself to the surgery.

"Good luck!" I called as they wheeled him out of the room.

At first, I didn't think he'd heard me, but then he raised his arm in acknowledgment. The gesture was probably as close to a thank-you as the lieutenant could get.

I knew he was going to have a tough road ahead of him. His attitude and unwillingness to follow a healthy regimen would make it even tougher. I wondered what it would be like to face such a major health crisis without any close relatives or dear friends to count on for comfort and practical help. At least, the lieutenant had Dawn and Dave. I felt fairly sure that they were his only friends.

As I walked down the hall toward the elevator, I pulled out my phone and called Dave at the station.

"I think I've solved the mystery of Jill," I told him when he answered. Then I explained that Samantha, the nurse who'd come by to help prep the lieutenant for surgery, must look a lot like Jill had when she was younger. "I could tell the lieutenant realized his mistake as soon as she pointed to her name tag. This woman is young; Jill Durand would be in her fifties by now."

"Just a coincidence. It sounds as though it has nothing to do with Ulysses's case."

"I suppose not, but I do wonder whether Jill could be involved somehow."

"I'll look into it, but according to Olivia, Ulysses hadn't had any contact with his ex-wife for years. Most likely, she's out of the picture. Anyway, thanks for letting me know. By the way, Dawn will be keeping tabs on Bill throughout the day, but he'll be in the ICU for at least twenty-four hours after surgery, so at least that'll keep him out of my hair for a while. He still thinks he should be in charge of the case."

Perhaps it wouldn't be such a bad idea, after all, for Dave to discuss the case with the lieutenant in a few days when he was up to it. It might take the lieutenant's mind off his health problems, temporarily at least.

On the way home, I made two stops, one at the bank and another at the supermarket, where I stocked up for the week. Flush with cash from the unexpected sale of my original painting to Brian, I spent twice as much for groceries as usual, and I had so many items to put away when I arrived home that my small pantry was bursting, and I had to ask Belle if I could borrow some freezer space because I couldn't fit everything into my dinky freezer.

"Do you still have those photocopies of the newspaper articles about Jill's disappearance?" I asked Belle as soon as we'd stowed my excess frozen food in her freezer.

"Sure, over here." She pulled a folder out of one of her kitchen drawers.

I opened the folder and put the article with the picture of Jill on the sunny countertop so that we could see it more clearly.

"I'm just trying to see the resemblance between her and that nurse Samantha." I'd already filled Belle in on my trip to the hospital.

"The picture looks so grainy," Belle complained. "Plus it's just a photocopy."

"I'd say there's some resemblance, but it's kind of hard to tell."

"Anyway, the woman you saw can't possibly be Jill. She's way too young. You said yourself that Sergeant Martinez thought it was just a coincidence."

"Yes, but for both Ulysses and Lieutenant Belmont to mistake her for Jill, she must look very much like Ulysses's ex-wife. What if she never forgave him? What if she's been harboring a desire for revenge all these years?"

"But you just said she couldn't possibly be Jill."

"No, she's not Jill. But she could be Jill's daughter."

Chapter 27

"Now you really have gone off the deep end. You don't even know whether Jill *has* a daughter, let alone whether she's nursing a decades-old grudge."

"It could make sense, though. Just think about it. Samantha works at the hospital. Nobody would think twice about seeing a nurse go into Ulysses's hospital room. Not only that, but I bet she's strong. She'd have to lift patients as part of her job. I think she has enough strength to strangle someone. She could have even given him a sedative earlier. Who knows?"

"That's quite a theory, but it's all speculation. There's no proof that this nurse had anything to do with Ulysses's murder. You said yourself that you and Dave both thought it was a coincidence that she resembles Jill. It doesn't have to mean anything more."

"True, but it could."

"Amanda Trent, what are you up to? I can see the wheels turning."

"Oh, just thinking. Maybe we should try to find out exactly who nurse Samantha is. It shouldn't be too difficult."

"What's this 'we'?"

"Aren't you the least little bit curious?"

"I guess so, but I still say your theory is far-fetched."

"You're probably right," I conceded, "but it couldn't hurt to check."

"What do you have in mind?"

"I have an idea, but let me think about it, and I'll call you later."

"OK. I know there's no stopping you, so keep me in the loop."

"I will. I promise."

I speculated that it shouldn't be too difficult to check on Samantha and find out more about her background. A woman in her twenties probably would have all sorts of social media profiles, but before I could check on those, I'd have to find out her last name. The nurses' name tags displayed only first names. That could be a deliberate strategy on the part of the hospital to protect their privacy.

Before planning a way to find out Jill's last name, I remembered that I needed to contact the buyers of the Siamese cats pet portrait. I wondered whether or not they intended to take delivery of the painting they had commissioned a couple of months earlier. Since they hadn't responded to my email or the online invoice I'd sent them through PayBuddy, I decided a phone call was in order at this point.

My customer apologized profusely for not getting back to me earlier. She and her family had been vacationing and hadn't been keeping up with email. I was pleased when she expressed satisfaction with her pets' portrait, but not so pleased when she asked me to have it framed and bill her for the framing. As patiently as I could, I explained that I didn't do any framing but that I could deliver the portrait to a local frame shop after she paid my invoice. I suggested Brooks's new enterprise at the resort, referring her to the shop's online gallery where a potential customer could upload an image and see how it would look with different framing and matting options. She seemed quite enthusiastic about the idea and told me she would try it out and let me know. I hoped she did decide to avail herself of the frame shop's services because it would be far easier for me to drop off the portrait in Lonesome Valley than to drive to Phoenix to a shipping company that specialized in shipping fine art all over the world. Once I delivered it to the frame shop, they would take on the responsibility of shipping the framed portrait to the customers.

Later, when I went into the studio to work, Mona Lisa surprised me by following Laddie. She stalked around the room as though she were hunting, but, finding no prey, she retreated to the living room. She seldom came into the studio, but every once in a while, she checked it out for some reason, known only to her.

I worked steadily for a couple of hours while Laddie stretched out on his bed and took an afternoon nap. I put my brush down and stepped back a few feet to gain a different perspective on my artwork, a rather cool expressionistic landscape done mostly in the hues of blue and green. I hoped to evoke a feeling of calmness with this particular painting, but I wasn't sure I was succeeding.

A knock on the studio door interrupted my reverie. When I saw Chip standing outside, I thought about the times he'd shown up unannounced, leaving me a bit on edge, shortly after I'd been accepted as a member of the Roadrunner. He hadn't come over lately, and I'd never invited him, but since he'd toned down his attempts to flirt with me, I didn't think he had flirtation on his mind today.

"Hey, Beautiful," he said breezily when I opened the door. Of course, Laddie was right behind me with a tail-wagging greeting of his own.

"You're just in time," I told him.

"I like the sound of that," he countered.

"I need your opinion on this landscape," I said, pointing to the canvas I'd been painting.

Despite his lighthearted bantering, Chip took art seriously, and I knew he'd give me an honest answer. I held my breath as he cast a critical eye on my landscape.

"It says serenity to me," he declared. "I like it."

"Not too moody?"

"No, I don't get that vibe at all. Is that what you're going for?"

"No, just quiet."

"You're nailing it."

"Thanks. It's always good to have another opinion. Sometimes I'm not too sure I'm succeeding."

"I know the feeling well. It's the bane of most artists. Deep down, we're often asking ourselves if our latest work is any good."

"I suppose that's true. Thanks for your insight, but I know you didn't come here to critique my painting. What's up?"

"It's Ralph. I'm worried about the old guy. I've taken him a pizza for dinner a couple of times, and I don't think he's taking care of himself. The larder was bare when I showed up at his house last night, and he's still having problems getting around. He was using a walker, instead of his cane, yesterday. I was going to ask Aunt Susan to check on him because she knows him a lot better than I do, but she's tied up getting ready for a couple of workshops she's leading in Phoenix tomorrow. And I can't very well contact Pamela. Her husband would probably go ballistic if he found out I'd called her."

"You want me to visit him to see how we can help."

"That's about the size of it. The problem is that he's a proud man. He insisted on paying for the pizzas I brought him—that part's OK, I guess, since he can afford it—but I definitely got the impression that he didn't want me around. Maybe this situation needs a woman's touch."

"OK. I could take him dinner tonight and offer to grocery shop for him."

"Good. I was hoping you'd say 'yes.'"

"Sure. I'll make a casserole, salad, and a dessert, enough for a couple of meals at least, and I'll offer to pick up whatever he needs at the supermarket."

"Hello?" a voice from outside called. Chip had left the door open, and I could see Brian standing in the doorway. As he stepped inside, he looked at Chip and me quizzically. "I'm sorry to interrupt," he said.

"You're not. Brian, this is Chip Baxter. He's one of the members of the Roadrunner. Chip, Brian's my next-door neighbor."

The two men shook hands.

"Nice to meet you, Brian," Chip said. "I need to get to work now. Thanks for your help, Amanda. Let me know how it goes."

"I will."

Chip gave Laddie a goodbye pat before Laddie trotted over to Brian, looking for attention from our latest visitor. Brian set a catalog he'd been carrying down on my desk and began to scratch behind Laddie's ears. Naturally, my eager dog made the most of his latest opportunity as he panted happily.

"I got this catalog in the mail last week, and I was about to pitch it when I remembered Belle's suggestions about adding some, uh, matching stuff to my living room."

"Accessories?"

"That's right. I suppose you can tell I don't know what I'm doing when it comes to setting up housekeeping. I never bothered with more than the basics when I lived in my apartment in Phoenix, but now that I have a house, I figure it should look like a home. Anyway, I dog-eared some pages in the catalog. I wonder if you'd mind taking a look and letting me know if I'm on the right track."

"Of course," I said, picking up the catalog and turning to the first page he'd turned down.

"Would these pillows work? I know Belle said to match colors in the painting, but I'm not too good at that. The tan pillows look like they'd match the sofa, though." He looked at me hopefully.

"Yes, they would, but using some pops of color around the room could liven it up a lot." I flipped through the next pages and found a good selection of pillows in a wide range of colors and sizes. "These, for example—two of the aquamarine and two smaller tangerine cushions—would brighten the room without overpowering your painting."

"All right. You're the expert. I'll order those." He stopped scratching Laddie long enough to circle the listing I'd suggested in the catalog. Laddie stood on his haunches, curling his front paws under his chin, and we both laughed at his antics.

"It's OK, Laddie," I said, as I petted him. "We haven't forgotten you."

I turned to Brian. "He's awfully good at soaking up attention, as you can see."

"I don't blame him," Brian replied. As soon as the words were out of his mouth, he turned beet red and made a beeline for the door.

Chapter 28

Brian's abrupt departure seemed a little odd. He hadn't even said goodbye, but I guessed he'd felt embarrassed. It was probably just as well that he hadn't lingered because, now that I'd offered to take Ralph dinner, I had to not only prepare the food but also figure out the best way to approach Jill.

As I assembled the ingredients for a chicken-and-rice casserole, I decided on a simple ruse, but I needed to find out what time the nurses' day shift ended at the hospital to time my visit with Ralph. I picked up my phone to call Belle.

"You don't happen to know what time the nurses at the hospital change shifts, do you?"

"No, but I can probably find out. I know a few people who work there."

"Great." I explained my simple plan to Belle, and she insisted on coming with me to the hospital when it was time to put my plan into action. I also told her about my more immediate mission to check on Ralph's welfare.

"We'll figure out our timing when we find out when the shift changes. Right now, I'm up to my elbows in chicken and rice."

"I'll let you know as soon as I find out."

I'd baked the casserole, prepared the salad, and whipped up my own shortcut version of chocolate mousse by the time Belle called me back.

"Sorry that took so long, but I hadn't talked to my friend Darlene in ages, and I thought it best to work my question about the shift changes casually into our conversation. Anyway, she told me they work twelve-hour shifts and change at seven, morning and evening."

"All right. I'll take Ralph's dinner to him early, around five. Then, I'll come back and pick you up. That should give us plenty of time to catch nurse Samantha before she leaves for the day. I can bring you home then, unless you need to go to the supermarket; I promised Chip I'd pick up some supplies for Ralph. He said it looked like he didn't have any food in the house."

"I'll tag along with you to the grocery store. I always have a list going, so I can do some shopping. Bring Laddie over when you're ready to go."

"Dennis won't mind?"

"No, he always likes to play with the dogs. He says it's relaxing after a day at the feed store."

It wasn't long before it was time to go to Ralph's, so I dropped off Laddie and told Belle I'd be back for her as soon as I could. I put Ralph's address in my phone so my GPS genie could direct me to his house. I'd been there only once before, and Susan had been driving, so I hadn't really paid attention to our route. I put the casserole in a sturdy box in the back of my SUV and carefully placed the salad and dessert in insulated containers on the passenger-side floor.

Before long, I was pulling into Ralph's driveway. He lived in a large ranch-style home, and his studio was in a separate building at the back of the property. Except for a few weeds poking through the light pea gravel in the front yard, nothing looked amiss.

I took the casserole out of the back and followed the winding sidewalk to the front door. Reminding myself to be patient since Ralph probably wouldn't be moving too quickly, if he was using a walker, I rang the bell and waited for him to appear. After several minutes, Ralph opened the door.

"Amanda, come on in," he invited me.

"Chip said your arthritis is bothering you, so I thought you might like a home-cooked meal."

"Great. Thank you. The kitchen's through here." Ralph led me through the living room and dining area to a large kitchen. He seemed happy enough at my visit. Maybe Chip had pegged the situation accurately, and Ralph would accept help more easily from a woman than from a man.

"Nice kitchen," I commented as I set the casserole down on the counter.

"I remodeled about ten years ago. Doubt that I'll have to do it again," he said ruefully.

I couldn't think of a good response to his comment, so I opted for concentrating on the task at hand. "I left a salad and some dessert in the car. Let me run out and get them, and I'll be right back."

"Use the kitchen door. It'll be closer."

When I went outside, I found myself only a few yards away from where I'd parked next to the house, but I hadn't seen the side door because of a large shrub that was blocking my view.

After retrieving the dishes, I returned to the house. "The casserole's only slightly warm," I told Ralph. "Let me pop it into the oven for about fifteen minutes, and it should be just right."

Ralph nodded, and I turned on the oven.

"I'll stick the salad and dessert in the fridge." Before Ralph had time to object, I'd opened the refrigerator door. Chip had been right. Except for some condiments, it was empty.

"It looks like it's time to stock up. I'm going to the supermarket later this evening. I might as well pick up whatever you need while I'm there. Let's make a list."

"All right, but I insist on paying for the groceries. And let me give you something for your time and trouble, too."

"You can pay for the groceries, but I assure you it's no trouble, and I have plenty of time, so groceries only. I insist."

As Ralph and I sat at his kitchen table making a shopping list, I congratulated myself that my take-charge attitude had paid off. When we finished, Ralph started to get up, but winced with pain and dropped back into his chair.

"Can I get you some medication?"

"Yeah, right there on the window sill above the sink."

"One or two?"

"Better make it two."

I handed him two tablets with a glass of water, and he downed the pills.

"I was just going to grab my checkbook, but if you wouldn't mind—"

"Sure. Where is it?"

"In the den." He gestured toward an arched doorway. "I think I left it on the coffee table. If not, it'll be on top of the desk."

"Be right back."

I found the checkbook on the coffee table, just as Ralph had said, but it wasn't the checkbook that caught my eye. There, hanging above the sofa, was the same painting I'd recognized in Ulysses's gallery show.

The same painting, but with one important difference—the artist's signature in the lower right corner read "Ralph Anderson."

Ulysses had ripped off Ralph's painting! Not only that, but he'd also licensed the image for commercial sales. That's how my mother had come to buy her jigsaw puzzle. I probably wouldn't have remembered the picture so clearly if seeing Ulysses's painting in his show hadn't jogged my memory eventually, although at the time I couldn't remember where I'd seen it before.

I realized Ralph must be aware of what Ulysses had done, but he hadn't said anything about it at the gallery reception. I wondered if Ulysses had made some kind of a deal with Ralph. I intended to find out, and there was only one way to do it.

I returned to the kitchen, laid Ralph's checkbook on the table, and sat down across from him. The look on my face must have given me away.

"You saw the painting, didn't you?" Ralph asked.

"Yes. What's the story, Ralph? How is it that your painting is in Ulysses's show with his name on it?"

"He copied it, brushstroke for brushstroke. I painted it the summer Ulysses was one of the students in my class. He was very talented as far as his technical skills, and he could copy anything, but when it came to the composition of an original work, Ulysses struggled."

"You mean you allowed Ulysses to copy your painting as an exercise?"

"No, I certainly did not. I didn't know he'd copied that piece until years later."

"What did you do when you found out?"

"Nothing," Ralph said with a sigh. "I was in a fairly deep depression at the time, and it was all I could do to keep going for the sake of my children. My wife had died after a long illness, and I was just about at the end of my rope, with the bills flooding in and trying to take care of the kids. I hadn't painted a thing in over a year, and I hadn't taught any classes, either. I didn't have the mental or emotional energy to pursue a case against Ulysses."

"I'm sorry you went through all that. Obviously, you were able to turn it around at some point."

"Finally, I realized that if I didn't do something, my kids would starve. My art business was kaput, and I knew it would take a long time to revive it. My health insurance had been canceled, too, and my family needed it, so I decided to get a job. I worked in the county assessor's office for years. I didn't get back to painting for quite a while after I started work, not till the kids were grown and gone."

"It sounds as though you did what you needed to do."

"I think so. I don't regret it."

"But what about Ulysses's copying your painting? That's not right."

"After all I'd been through, I never pursued it. I suppose I could have sued him, but, by that time, years had passed. He'd made a name for himself. It's entirely possible that he could have convinced a jury that I had copied his painting, rather than the other way around."

"You never said anything to Ulysses about it?"

"I hadn't seen or talked to Ulysses since he took summer art classes from me. I wondered how he'd react when he saw me at his show's opening."

"He acted as though you were long-lost friends."

"Believe me, we were never friends."

Chapter 29

"I don't know whether you remember him, but Lieutenant Belmont told me you let Ulysses stay in your studio a couple of times after his wife called the police because he hit her."

"Bill Belmont? I know who he is, mainly because the chief mentions him once in a while."

I'd forgotten that Ralph and Lonesome Valley's police chief were friends.

"Anyway, I let him stay in the studio a couple of times, although I warned him I wouldn't put up with his behavior after the second incident, talented student or not."

"Did you know Ulysses's wife Jill?"

"Not well. What I remember most is the day she disappeared from our plein air paint-out. Ulysses was frantic until he found out she'd taken the opportunity to leave him while he was busy painting at the event."

"Whatever became of her, I wonder."

"I don't know. When he came back to class later, he acted embarrassed and he never mentioned her again."

As we talked, I removed the casserole from the oven and set it on a trivet on the kitchen table. I found a plate in the cupboard and silverware in a drawer and set them in front of Ralph.

"Say, you don't have to wait on me. I can fend for myself."

"I know, but I'm almost done," I said, as I tossed the salad and placed a generous serving in a bowl for Ralph. Setting a ramekin of chocolate mousse next to the salad, I pronounced, "There you go."

"Thanks, Amanda. Everything looks good, and I do appreciate it."

"I'll be on my way now, but it might be a while before I come back with your groceries. I need to stop back home to pick up my next-door neighbor first." I didn't mention our planned stop at the hospital.

I'd stayed a little bit longer at Ralph's house than I'd anticipated, but Belle and I still had plenty of time to catch up with Samantha before her shift ended. I called Belle before starting my SUV to let her know I was on the way.

She was outside at the curb, waiting for me when I arrived, and we headed to the hospital.

A couple of cars were exiting the hospital's parking lot when we arrived, so I turned into the front lot in hopes of snagging a spot that had just been vacated. We were in luck.

"This is the first time I've been able to park right out front," I told Belle.

"Things should improve after the new parking garage is finished," Belle commented.

We planned on heading up to the fourth floor and engaging Samantha in conversation. I thought I could remind her that I'd seen her in Lieutenant Belmont's room earlier in the day and ask her about his condition as an opener.

Before we reached the hospital's main entrance, we spotted Dawn and Dave coming out of the building.

"Hi, Amanda," Dawn greeted me. "If you're here to check

on Bill, we were just up at the ICU. He's doing all right, but they wouldn't let us visit him. They'll be moving him back to his room tomorrow." She turned to Belle. "I'm sorry I don't remember your name."

"Belle Compton. We met a few months ago. My husband and my dog were with me. Amanda's dog, too."

"Oh, sure. That was quite a night." I'd solved a murder that evening, quite by accident, and Lieutenant Belmont never forgave me for it.

Dave looked at us, as though expecting us to turn around to leave now that they'd told us that Lieutenant Belmont couldn't have any visitors today, so I told him that the gift shop was featuring my scarves and that we wanted to check on sales. Of course, I'd only just dropped off the new stock this morning, so I doubted that there'd been any sales in the meantime, but I didn't want to tell Dave about our real mission in visiting the hospital. He already thought that nurse Samantha's resemblance to Jill was nothing more than a coincidence, and I didn't believe he'd appreciate my efforts to find out more about her. Anyway, as Belle had said, my idea about her being Jill's daughter could be way off base. It was little more than a hunch, really.

When we entered the lobby, Belle nudged me. "Let's check your scarf display."

"OK, but I doubt anything's been sold since this morning."

There was a different staffer, a woman I'd never seen before, in the gift shop this evening. Belle went straight to the scarf display, and the clerk said, "Those are really popular. I sold two this afternoon, and I'm going to buy one myself. I'm just trying to decide which color I want."

When I let her know I'd made the scarves, she told me how

much she liked them. As we left, Belle smiled. "I'd say it's going pretty well."

"Thanks to you and Dennis. Your display idea really helped."

"I'm glad. I'm going to ask Dennis to make another display stand. Then we can pitch some boutiques."

"That would be great," I said, as I walked toward the elevator. "I have to get busy and dye more scarves. After delivering the gift shop's order, I have just enough of them left to display in the studio for tours."

"Which floor?" a white-coated man asked as we boarded the elevator.

"Fourth, please."

We must have come at peak visiting time, I thought, as we squeezed into the crowded elevator, but by the time it reached the fourth floor, half of its occupants had departed.

We went straight to the nursing station where I asked for Samantha, explaining that I'd seen her earlier in the day and I wanted to talk to her.

"Sorry, you've missed her. She worked half a shift today. Can I help you?"

"No, that's OK." I didn't want to say anything to make the other nurses suspicious. "I'll try to catch her tomorrow, when I come back to visit my friend."

"She won't be here. She's not scheduled to work again until Friday."

"All right. Friday, then." I tried to sound casual. The less I said, the better. If they thought I was trying to find out personal information about her, they might warn her off.

We hadn't accomplished our mission at the hospital, but, at least, we'd learned when Samantha would be back on duty. I hated to wait until Friday to talk to her, but there didn't seem to be any alternative.

When we arrived at the supermarket, Belle and I both grabbed carts and proceeded aisle-by-aisle to shop the store. Since I'd already done my grocery shopping for the week in the morning, I concentrated exclusively on Ralph's list, while Belle filled her cart. The store wasn't very busy, and we were able to check out without waiting in a long line. Belle had brought her own cloth bags, so we wouldn't have any difficulty knowing which groceries to unload at Ralph's.

Outside lights blazed from above his garage door as I pulled into the well-illuminated driveway. The winding sidewalk to the front door was lined with more discreet light fixtures that had a subtle glow.

Belle and I both picked up a couple of bags. Since I now knew where the side door was located, I tapped on that. Ralph must have been waiting in the kitchen because it didn't take him nearly as long to answer the door as it had earlier.

He stepped back after opening the door, and we put the bags on the kitchen countertop. Before making another trip to the SUV for the rest of the groceries, I introduced Belle and Ralph. He took his right hand off the walker and held it out to shake hands with her. I noticed she winced a bit as they shook.

"For someone who has arthritis, he has quite a grip," she told me when we went back to the SUV to retrieve the rest of the groceries.

"His pain is worse some days than others. He told me sometimes it's so bad, he can't hold a brush to paint."

"That must be awful for an artist as accomplished as he is."

I nodded. I knew I'd feel terribly frustrated if I wasn't able to paint, and I was sure Ralph felt the same way.

Back inside, Ralph told us where to stash everything, and we made short work of putting the food away. We didn't linger afterwards since Belle had some cold items in her bags and she'd need to refrigerate them soon.

Laddie and Mr. Big greeted us joyfully at Belle's, and Dennis quickly grabbed our grocery bags so that we could pet our excited canines.

"They should sleep well tonight," he said. "Laddie chased his ball for a long time, and Mr. Big chased Laddie. They both ought to feel exhausted, even though they've been napping while I made you another scarf display, Amanda."

"I was going to ask you to do that," Belle said. "Great minds think alike," she added, as she kissed him.

"Thanks so much, Dennis. The first one we took to the hospital gift shop made all the difference. I don't know that the shop would be selling them right now if not for you."

Dennis beamed. "You know I'm always happy to help, and I bet I know someone else who'd be more than willing to lend a hand, too."

"Who?"

"Your other next-door neighbor, Brian. I get the feeling he likes you."

"What did I tell you, Amanda?" Belle piped up. "I'm not the only one who's noticed."

I supposed I'd have to concede that Brian's odd, sudden discomfiture and abrupt departure from my studio in the afternoon might mean something. Perhaps he *was* interested in me.

I didn't know whether I was ready for that kind of attention from a man. Although it had been a little over a year since Ned had divorced me, the time had flown, and, once in a while, it seemed like only yesterday. I'd been hurt, and I didn't want to be hurt again. I was happy with the new life I'd created in Lonesome Valley, and I wasn't sure I wanted anything more. On the other hand, I wasn't sure I should rule it out, either.

"What do *you* think, boy?" I asked Laddie, as we walked home across Belle's front yard, but his only response was his wagging tail.

Chapter 30

By mid-morning the next day, I was fretting that my customer who'd commissioned the painting of her Siamese cats still had not paid my PayBuddy invoice. I was debating whether to contact her when she called me to let me know that she'd found the perfect frame online from the resort's frame shop, and they would be expecting me to drop off the portrait today. I replied that I'd be happy to do that as soon as I received payment for it. This statement provoked a flurry of apologies from my customer, who promised to take care of it right away. I was pleasantly surprised to find she had done so when I checked my email and found a notification from PayBuddy that money had been deposited to my account. Since she'd paid me, my incipient irritation with her vanished. I emailed her a thank-you message and promised to let her know as soon as I delivered the portrait safely to the frame shop.

Although I'd planned on working on my painting, I decided it would be a better idea to deliver the pet portrait to the frame shop right away. I didn't plan to be gone long, but I put a treat in both Laddie's and Mona Lisa's bowls in the kitchen to distract them from my imminent departure. Of course, Laddie wasn't fooled, and Mona Lisa probably didn't care one way or the other, but it made me feel better, even though I knew perfectly well that they could cope on their own for a few hours.

Carefully, I secured the Siamese cats portrait in the back of my SUV so that it wouldn't slide around. I drew a few stares from people shopping at the resort's mall as I carried it toward the frame shop, but most of them were too busy peeking into the windows of the high-end shops that lined the mall to notice me.

I entered the frame shop and headed toward the counter. I didn't see anybody inside, but there was a back room where the actual framing was done, so I assumed somebody would come to the front to assist me in short order. As I walked toward the counter, passing the doorway that connected the frame shop and the Brooks Miller Gallery next door, I was literally blindsided and knocked to the floor.

If I'd heard someone coming toward me, perhaps I would have had a chance to react and protect the painting, but, as it was, it had flown out of my hands when I'd been knocked down. I was so dazed for a minute that I lay there, trying to assess the damage. I'd gone down hard on the tile floor. Both my knees were protesting, and my right wrist didn't feel much better. I looked up and, for the first time, saw who'd run into me.

Groaning, I slowly got to my feet, looking toward the painting that had flown out of my hands, rather than at Gabrielle, who'd knocked me down. She must have been coming into the frame shop at a pretty good clip to have hit me so hard, I thought.

Instead of apologizing, she blamed me. "How could you be so clumsy?" she demanded.

"Now, wait just a second! You ran into *me*. I didn't even see you coming."

"You should watch where you're going," she sneered.

"I saw what happened," a deep voice proclaimed. "You're the one who should be apologizing."

Brooks had come out of the back room and was glaring at his wife.

"That does it!" Gabrielle snapped. "I can't believe you'd take her side. Why is she always hanging around, anyway?"

"I have business here," I said, picking up the portrait to examine it. If the painting had been damaged, I'd feel even angrier at Gabrielle than I did already.

Brooks came over, took the portrait from me, and placed it on the counter. "It looks like one corner took the brunt," he said, "but it's not too bad. We can repair it."

"That's typical of you, Brooks," Gabrielle complained. "You care more for everybody else than you do for me."

Brooks ignored her comment. "I believe you owe our customer an apology. You ran into *her*."

"Unbelievable! That proves what I said. You couldn't care less about me."

"I've tried to accommodate you in every way I can. I've stood by while you acted like a spoiled brat and supported you because you're my wife, but I've had it up to here with your petty bad behavior and your tantrums."

"You're just like Ulysses. He never gave any credit to Olivia, and you never give any credit to me. If I hadn't been your gallery manager in your downtown location, you never would have sold any of your awful art."

I drew in my breath, shocked that Gabrielle would tell Brooks his artwork was bad. Granted, she wasn't wrong, and I suspected that Brooks realized it now, too, although, when he owned the old gallery, I believe he'd truly thought he was a great artist. He'd obviously changed course in his career in the art world, shifting from studio artist to art gallery owner, so it was nothing other than downright mental cruelty for Gabrielle to tell her husband his artwork was bad at this late stage, after he'd already forsaken it.

Brooks looked as stunned as if she'd smacked him in the face, but Gabrielle continued, oblivious to his reaction to her rant. "You promised me the moon when we met in New York, but this isn't what I signed up for. I do all the work, and you take all the credit."

"That's not fair, and you know it. I've given you everything you ever asked for."

"No way. You don't appreciate me at all. I was better off in New York. This hick town is the pits. They roll up the sidewalks at six o'clock around here. We haven't even gone to a nightclub all year. I can't take it anymore. I'm out of here."

"What do you mean?"

"What I mean is I'm leaving you! I'm going back to New York. You'll be hearing from my lawyers. I'm getting a divorce!"

With that shocking announcement, Gabrielle turned on her six-inch Louboutin heel and stalked off.

I thought Brooks might go after her, but he stayed in the frame shop and proceeded to examine the Siamese cats portrait more closely.

Much as I felt like slinking out, I knew I needed to make sure the painting could be repaired and properly framed, despite the damage. I couldn't just go on to business, though. Awkward as it might be, I felt I should acknowledge the scene I'd just witnessed.

"Brooks, I'm sorry. Maybe you should go after Gabrielle." Although I thought Gabrielle was behaving badly and her reaction to his suggestion that she apologize to me had seemed extreme, she *was* Brooks's wife. Perhaps she'd cool down before taking steps to leave Brooks and divorce him.

"Don't be sorry," he said. "She may be fed up with me, but I'm fed up with her, too. She's spoiled and unpleasant to be around most of the time. I put up with it because she's a beautiful woman, but there's a limit to what I'll tolerate from her or anybody else. This has been building for a long time. It has nothing to do with what just happened here, and, by the way, I'm the one who's sorry. I apologize to you for the way she's acted toward you, while I stood by and never said a word."

"Thank you," I murmured, rubbing my throbbing wrist.

We turned our attention back to the painting, and Brooks assured me again that they could repair the damage, and it would look perfect in the frame my customer had selected. He wrote me a receipt for delivery and confirmed that the frame shop would take on the responsibility of shipping the painting to the customer.

My right knee hurt so badly as I walked back through the mall that I was limping. I knew both knees would be turning black and blue. I'd hit the tiled floor in the frame shop hard, and I still felt shaky from the incident. I never could fathom why Gabrielle had always ignored me, although she certainly hadn't done that today. After hearing what Brooks had said about his own wife, I thought the explanation might be as simple as the fact that she wasn't a very nice person, one Brooks was probably better off without.

Gabrielle had been awfully quick to say that she was returning to New York. I was betting she'd already made plans to leave Brooks and Lonesome Valley behind and had been looking for an excuse to announce her departure. Or maybe she'd come into the frame shop intending to tell Brooks she was going to divorce him and I happened to get in her way.

After I left the resort, I sat in my SUV for a few minutes, trying to calm down, because, now that I thought about it, I was even angrier that Gabrielle had knocked me to the floor and then blamed me for getting in her way. I remembered that, only a few months ago, Dustin had been so taken with her beauty that he'd asked her out. Luckily, nothing had come of that date, since he'd canceled it when he'd found out that she was married. He'd dodged a bullet there, I thought. I couldn't say I was sorry to see her leave town.

After I steadied myself a bit, I started the car and headed to the hospital. Lieutenant Belmont should have been moved back into his room by now, and, although I didn't look forward to sparring with the grumpy lieutenant, I wanted to find out whether he could tell me more about Jill.

When I arrived at the hospital, I stopped at the reception desk in the lobby to confirm that Lieutenant Belmont had been moved back to his room. If he was still in the ICU, I wouldn't be able to visit him, but, since the receptionist gave me 402 as his room number, I boarded the elevator and went to the fourth floor.

The lieutenant's eyes were closed when I entered his room, and he lay very still. I thought he must be asleep, so I began to tiptoe toward the door, but he startled me by coughing and then raising his bed so that he sat up. He looked ghastly pale.

"Don't ask. I feel terrible."

It was difficult to know what to say to him. I knew he had a long road ahead of him, and his attitude wouldn't make it any easier.

"You're only a day out of surgery. Give it some time. Can I

get you that glass of water now?"

He glared at me and burst out laughing. "No water, but I could sure go for that cheeseburger you wouldn't bring me the other day."

"Ha ha. You know I can't do that."

At least he hadn't lost his spunk.

"Well, OK," he said grudgingly. "Maybe next time. How about making yourself useful and watering that scraggly plant you brought me? It looks worse than I feel."

"I can do that." I poured some water from the pitcher into an extra cup and dribbled it slowly onto the soil around the plant. It did look a little droopy, but it certainly wasn't scraggly.

When I finished, I sat down in a chair beside his bed.

"Remember that nurse you called Jill right before your surgery?"

"Yeah, what of it?"

"Ulysses thought he'd seen Jill, too. Of course, she couldn't be Jill; she's too young, but do you know whether or not Jill has a daughter?"

"No idea," he said, but he suddenly looked more alert than he had earlier. "She looked just like Jill, though. It's uncanny." He paused. "Funny that I should remember her so well after so long."

"Did you ever see her again after you located her in Sedona?"

"Nope. That was it. You think the nurse bumped off Ulysses as some kind of revenge for the way he treated her mother?"

"The thought had occurred to me."

"Unlikely. We don't know that Jill and the nurse are even related."

"But what if they are? Either one of them could have a motive, but the nurse—Samantha's her name—also had the means and opportunity. She could have sedated Ulysses before she strangled him, and he wouldn't have known what was happening."

"Whoa! Slow down. That might be a bridge too far."

"Maybe, but it's worth checking on, don't you think?"

Chapter 31

"Does Dave know what you're up to?"

"I spoke with him about Samantha. At the time, we both thought that it was an odd coincidence that both you and Ulysses said she looked like Jill. He did tell me that he planned to look into Jill, though."

"Makes sense," he said thoughtfully. "Ex-spouse and all. I'll see what I can get out of him when he and Dawn come to visit me tonight."

"Will you keep me posted?"

"Only if you keep *me* posted."

"I suppose it wouldn't hurt," I agreed, against my better judgment. I still felt bad that the lieutenant had suffered his life-altering heart attack in my living room. Besides, I told myself, the only time he seemed to forget his health problems was when he concentrated on a case. I knew Dawn and Dave wanted to keep him in the dark about any police business while he recuperated from his bypass surgery, so I felt somewhat guilty in encouraging his interest, but I rationalized that it was a potentially productive distraction for the dour lieutenant.

"See if you can track down Jill, and I'll find out what I can about Samantha."

The lieutenant seemed to enjoy bossing me around, but since his command aligned with my plans, anyway, I agreed.

"By the way," I told him, "nurse Samantha won't be back on duty until Friday, so you won't be able to talk to her until then."

"Checked on her schedule already, did you?" He looked at me with a hint of grudging approval. "No matter. I'll find out what we need to know before then. You just concentrate on finding Jill."

"You don't happen to remember the name of the restaurant in Sedona where you saw her last, do you?"

"Nope, but I know exactly where it was." He told me the location and insisted on drawing a map. "Not much to go on after all these years, but it's a place to start. I assume you've already tried to track her down online."

I nodded.

"Figures. Well, Dave might have more luck at that than you will. I'll see what I can get out of him when Dawn's not around."

I was fairly sure Dave Martinez wasn't going to share the details of his investigation with Lieutenant Belmont. The sergeant was convinced that the detective should remain in the dark while he recovered.

When I didn't respond, the lieutenant glowered at me. "Well, what are you waiting for? Get out of here, and let a dying man rest in peace."

I started to protest that he wasn't dying when I saw a shadow of a smirk cross his face.

"Yes, sir," I said with a straight face. I decided I might as well play along with him. At least the prospect of an investigation had captured his interest, and he'd perked up a bit.

By the time I arrived home, both my knees were swollen. I took an Ibuprofen and put some ice in a couple of sandwich bags, wrapped a hand towel around each, and sat on the sofa with my legs propped up and a bag of ice on each knee. Mona Lisa jumped on my lap and began meowing loudly, while Laddie sat beside me and rested his head against my leg. Mona Lisa didn't appreciate the competition, and I was lucky I sensed what was coming in time to prevent her from raking her claws over Laddie's nose. As it was, she took a swipe at him, but I deflected her paw, and she ended up scratching me instead.

"Ouch!" I exclaimed, as I picked her up and moved her away from Laddie. "Behave yourself."

She jumped onto my left shoulder before leaping down and stalking off to her perch. Meanwhile, Laddie crowded close to me, begging to be petted. "Sibling rivalry, huh, boy?" I murmured, as I obliged him for a few minutes. When I rose to tend to my latest wound, Laddie glanced at Mona Lisa with a see-she-likes-me-better-than-you look, and she hissed at him before turning her back to both of us.

Icing my knees and taking the pain medication helped, and I was no longer limping, so I decided to spend the afternoon in the studio, where I turned my attention to the unfinished pet portrait of a solemn bloodhound with soulful eyes. I'd neglected this one a bit, prioritizing the portrait of the Siamese cats because that order had been placed first, but I'd also worked on my latest landscape before getting back to the bloodhound whose name was Toby. Fortunately, I'd estimated I would finish Toby's portrait in mid-October, so I had plenty of time to finish it if only I'd stick to a more regular work schedule.

I'd already decided that I'd interrupt my painting the next

morning to drive to Sedona in hopes of picking up Jill's trail. I thought the chances of finding any clue to Jill's current whereabouts were quite slim, so, to justify the trip, I also planned to make a few sales calls to boutiques there in hopes of landing another wholesale account for my silk scarves.

After spending a few hours in the studio, I decided to call it quits. I'd made good progress, and Toby's portrait was shaping up very nicely, but my wrist had begun to throb again, and I thought it best to give it a rest.

I called Belle to let her know my plans. Although she wanted to come with me, she'd be doing her voluntary work in the library in the afternoon. Since there was a good chance the trip could run into the afternoon, she thought she should skip it. She asked me to drop Laddie off at her house when I was ready to leave so that he and Mr. Big could play. If I wasn't back by the time she had to leave for the library, she'd take Laddie back home, so the two dogs wouldn't be left to their own devices.

After an early dinner, I iced my knees again. Although they weren't especially bothering me, I thought it might keep the swelling down. By the time I returned my makeshift ice packs to my crowded freezer, I was feeling fairly good, and the evening was so pleasant that I decided to take Laddie for a walk. We could always turn around and come back if the pain started again, so, rather than heading toward the park and possibly disappointing Laddie if we had to turn back, I started off in the other direction, turning left when we reached the front sidewalk.

This way took us past Brian's house. I didn't really expect to see him outside, but his garage door was open, and I could see him at his workbench. He looked up as we crossed his driveway, hesitated for a few seconds, and then called to me.

We stopped, and Brian came out to greet us. Laddie whipped his tail back and forth when he saw Brian coming toward us, and my golden boy's tail moved even faster when Brian scratched him behind the ears.

"Out for a walk?" he asked.

"Yes, probably just a short one." I didn't tell him my reason for keeping it short. It would have been difficult to explain my accident without mentioning the argument it had sparked. Brian didn't know Gabrielle or Brooks, and I couldn't imagine that he'd have any interest in their domestic squabbles.

"Mind if I join you?"

"We don't mind." I smiled. "You're welcome to come along."

"Let me close the garage door." He returned to the garage, punched a code into the outside remote control, and the door rolled down and closed. He joined us, and we started walking at a leisurely stroll, rather than a brisk clip.

"It's nice that you have a garage. My carport's all right, but I hate to store things in it since it's open. I have to keep my microwave in there, though, because I really don't have room for it inside."

"You keep your microwave in the carport?"

"Oh, it's not the one I use for reheating food. I use it for setting the dye on the silk scarves I make. Otherwise, I'd have to steam-set them, and that's an even messier process." I realized I was getting a bit carried away. I doubted that Brian was interested in my methods of dying scarves.

"Oh, I see. You know you might consider enclosing your carport. It shouldn't be too big a job to finish it and install an automatic door."

"That sounds like a good idea, but I can't move it to my

priority list just yet." Even though Brian didn't view it as a big job, I thought it would most likely be a costly one, something I should put off until I could build up my savings, which were nil right at the moment. As it had been since the day I moved to Lonesome Valley, my focus remained making enough money to pay my bills every month.

"Maybe something to consider in the future," he said amiably. I was glad he didn't continue to push his idea. If it had been Ned, he never would have stopped trying to convince me to do what he wanted until I did it.

"What's it like living out in the middle of the ocean for half the year?" I asked, switching gears. "I'm curious." I'd never known someone who worked on an oil rig. Although the job sounded somewhat exotic, I was guessing that it had become routine for Brian.

"Well, it's different, all right. Obviously, we can't run out for fast food or go to the latest movie at the drop of a hat. It took me a while to get used to it, and the schedule has its drawbacks, but it has some benefits, too. When I'm working, it's easier to concentrate on getting the job done. There aren't the distractions that come with most jobs."

"I can understand that. I'm afraid I get distracted from my painting all too often. What else?"

"When I'm not on the rig, I'm off work. I mean I'm *really* off work. I don't think about it because I'm not there, and somebody else is covering the job while I'm home. There's a total separation between work and home, and I kind of like that because my job isn't my life. Not like you. You're an artist. You live your art every day."

"Wow! I guess that's true. I hadn't really thought about it that way, but my life really does revolve around my art now."

Chapter 32

Brian and I had a pleasant walk with Laddie. I learned that he'd worked on an oil rig from the time he'd graduated from community college, starting from the bottom and working his way up to his manager's job and earning his bachelor's degree online along the way. Every four weeks, he boarded a plane to Texas, and his company's helicopter flew the employees who were coming on duty out to the rig.

Although he'd mentioned his time was his own when he wasn't working, he hadn't really said what he liked to do. From the magazines and books I'd noticed on his coffee table the day he bought my landscape, I deduced that he was somewhat of a history buff. I'd also noticed lots of tools hanging on the wall above his garage workbench, so I thought he might have something in common with Dennis, who could fix just about anything around the house.

We walked a little farther than I'd intended, and my sore knees were starting to protest by the time we approached Brian's house. Brian noticed that I'd slowed down a bit.

"Are you all right, Amanda?"

"I'm fine. I had a bump on my knees earlier today, so they're a little bit sore."

"Anything I can do to help? I can walk Laddie for you tomorrow so you can rest."

"No, thanks, Brian. I appreciate the offer, but Belle's going to watch him tomorrow morning while I drive over to Sedona. I'm going to try to sell my scarves to some of the boutiques there."

"You're a busy lady. I hope you're not too busy to have dinner with me tomorrow night." When I hesitated, he added, "Or maybe you won't be back in time."

"I should be."

"Well?"

"Yes, of course. That would be nice."

I wasn't really sure that dinner was a good idea, but I couldn't think of a polite way of turning Brian down, and I didn't know that I wanted to, anyway. I kept going back and forth about it. There wasn't a doubt in my mind that Brian had asked me for a date. If we dated and decided to call it quits after a while, it would be more than awkward to be living right next door to him. He seemed like a nice guy, and he'd worded his suggestion for a dinner date so naturally into our conversation that he'd taken me by surprise.

"Great!" he said enthusiastically. "Pick you up at seven?"

"All right; I'll see you then." With a little wave, I bade him good-bye, and Laddie pranced along by my side the few yards to my house.

I debated with myself all evening about my upcoming date. I didn't know whether I should have agreed to it or not, but, since I had, it was too late to back out now. I would never stand somebody up—not unless an emergency prevented me from keeping a date, so I decided I might as well make the best of it. I couldn't decide what to wear. I looked through my closet and came away without making a decision. Dinner could just as easily mean a trip to the local pizza place as an upscale event at a fine restaurant, and Brian hadn't mentioned any particular eatery.

Later, when I went to bed, Mona Lisa and Laddie snuggled close, their earlier feud forgotten for now. I fell asleep without ever deciding on my ensemble.

Although I hated to do it, I had to call Belle early the next morning to remind her that I'd be bringing Laddie over to visit soon. Dennis answered the phone and assured me that Belle was already awake. As soon as I was ready, I put a few dog treats in a baggie so Laddie and Mr. Big could have a mid-morning snack. I had no idea how long I'd be gone, but, if I hadn't made any progress by mid-afternoon, I intended to come back home. It was about an hour's drive, so that would give me time to get ready for my dinner with Brian.

The aroma of coffee brewing wafted my way when Belle opened the door for Laddie and me. Mr. Big came running to greet his buddy, and the two dogs rolled around on the floor together in a joyful frenzy.

Belle, still in her robe, smiled. "I'm going to have my coffee on the patio while they play in the backyard," she said. "Do you have time for a cup?"

"I'd better get on the road. I'm not sure how long this is going to take."

"I wish I could come with you. Promise you'll call if you have any news, and be sure to let me know if you won't be home by five. I can pick up Laddie after I get home from the library."

"I should be back before then, but I'll keep you posted."

I hugged Laddie and told him to be a good boy. He was

always happy to stay with Mr. Big, so I left them to their doggy play date and went on my way.

I glanced at the map Lieutenant Belmont had drawn before I pulled out of the driveway. I had the address of a restaurant that was at the same intersection on the map, although it probably wasn't the same restaurant where Lieutenant Belmont had found Jill all those years ago, but it was a place to start. I'd searched on an online app to find the exact place that Lieutenant Belmont had marked, and, now that I'd put it into my GPS genie on my phone, I could head straight there as soon as I reached Sedona.

What should have been an hour's drive took half an hour longer than I'd anticipated due to an oversize motor home that was traveling well below the speed limit on the winding two-lane road. There was no place to pass, so I had to follow the huge vehicle for miles before reaching my destination.

When I came to the city limits, I turned on the GPS and followed directions to the corner where the restaurant stood. Evidently, it was a popular spot. There were people crowding in the door, and the parking lot was jammed. I waited until a man driving a black pickup truck pulled out, and I zipped into the vacated spot, earning a disgusted stare from a woman approaching from the other direction, but, since I hadn't cut her off, I didn't feel guilty in the slightest.

Inside, a hostess greeted me, and I could see that I was in for a wait. She took my name and told me she could seat me in about twenty minutes before escorting a group of four to their table. It was standing room only in the small area between the cash register and the door. I was planning to ask the hostess how long the restaurant had been in business, but she was so busy I didn't get a chance until she finally called my name and led me to a small, two-seater table near the back of the restaurant. As she handed me a menu, I learned that she'd been working at the place only a few months and had no idea how long it had been in business.

Since I'd already eaten breakfast before leaving home, I'd planned to limit my order to some tea, but I found I couldn't ignore the aroma of cinnamon rolls as a server carried a tray past me laden with cinnamon rolls so huge each covered a dinner plate.

When my server, a young woman whose blond hair was confined to a neat bun at the nape of her neck, approached me to take my order, I asked her if a smaller version of the sweet treat was available.

"Sure thing. We have a mini-bun. It's about this size," she said, forming a small circle with her fingers.

"OK. I'll have one of those and some tea." Then, I repeated the same question I'd asked the hostess, but my server didn't know the answer, either, so I went on to another question. "Do you happen to know if there's anybody around who's worked here a really long time? I'm looking for a woman who used to work here years ago."

"What's her name? I could ask in the kitchen."

"Jill Durand."

"Doesn't ring a bell, but I'll check with Tony. He's our baker."

I thanked her and waited for my order to be delivered. The cinnamon roll she set before me was oozing with glistening white frosting, and she set a small dish containing a generous dollop of butter next to it.

"Tea's still brewing," she said as she placed an empty cup on the table along with a cute little china pot decorated with the image of mischievous kittens playing with a ball of yarn.

"Tony gets off work in a few minutes," she said. "He can talk to you then."

"Oh, great!" I said. I was so surprised I'd have dropped my fork if I'd been holding it. I hadn't had high hopes that I'd be able to learn anything about Jill, but now it seemed I was on the verge of finding out what had become of her. As I ate my cinnamon roll, which I'd slathered with butter, I wondered how much Tony knew about Ulysses's ex-wife. I was sipping my tea when a portly man dressed in baker's whites came to my table and sat in the chair opposite me.

"Tia said you're looking for Jill Durand."

"That's right. Do you know her?"

"What do you want with Jill?" he asked cautiously, as though I might be a bill collector on her trail.

I decided to take the long way around in hopes of putting his mind at ease. I explained that I was an artist in Lonesome Valley and that I also made tie-dyed scarves and handed him my business cards—one for my art business and the other one for the silk scarf business.

He scanned both and immediately relaxed. At least, he knew I wasn't a debt collector.

"That one of your scarves?" he asked, motioning to the fuchsia silk scarf draped around my neck.

"Yes, it is. I use several different techniques to make abstract designs."

"Looks like something Beth might stock. Jill goes by 'Beth' now. You'll find her at the Desert Rose Boutique. It's about a mile down the road on the left-hand side. You can't miss it. It's the only rose-covered cottage on the block."

"Thank you, Tony. And thanks for the delicious cinnamon

roll, too. I understand you're the baker."

"Yup, thirty years here now. I've been through four owners, and the restaurant's changed names a few times, too, but the cinnamon rolls are the same as they were back then." He hefted himself up from the table. "Thirty years of starting work at two o'clock in the morning: you'd think I'd be tired of it by now, but I'm not quitting any time soon."

"I'm sure your customers would be happy to know that."

Frankly, I was astonished that Tony hadn't asked more questions—questions that would have been difficult to answer without arousing suspicion.

I couldn't believe my luck. Had Jill Durand lived in Sedona the whole time since she'd left Ulysses? If so, she'd been practically right under our noses, a mere hour's drive from Lonesome Valley. Close enough to visit Ulysses in the hospital. Close enough to murder him in his bed!

Chapter 33

Before getting out of my SUV, I debated whether I should lug the display stand in with me. After all, I planned to make this a legitimate sales call and try to engage Jill in a more far-reaching conversation in hopes of learning what I could about her. Finally, I decided to leave the display stand in the back of the SUV since it was a bit awkward to carry and probably wasn't the subtlest way of pitching my scarves.

I went inside, where I was immediately attracted to a lovely aubergine maxi dress with silver bugle beads accenting the neckline. Displayed on a mannequin, the elegant simplicity of the dress drew me to it. I felt the fabric, which was as beautiful as the dress's design. I took a peek at the price tag and dropped it like a hot potato.

"May I help you?"

I twirled around and could see immediately that the offer to assist me hadn't come from Jill, but from a young woman with wavy red hair. I introduced myself, explained my mission, and asked to see Jill.

The woman looked confused. "I'm sorry. Nobody by that name works here."

"My mistake," I said quickly. I took a small notebook out of my purse and pretended to consult it. "I meant Beth."

"She's not here right now." When I looked disappointed, she added, "But she should be back in a few minutes. She had to run to the bank. Would you like to try on that dress while you wait?" She looked me over appraisingly. "We have only two of them in stock, and I'm sure one of them is in your size."

"Well, yes, all right. I would like to try it on." What could it hurt? I asked myself. I had to kill some time before Jill returned. Besides, if it didn't look good on me, I wouldn't feel bad about not purchasing it.

The clerk located the dress on a nearby rack and led me to a small dressing room in the back of the boutique. She showed me the large mirrors outside the dressing room and encouraged me to come out to see my reflection in them from every angle as soon as I tried on the dress. It took me only a few minutes to shed my linen pants, jersey top, and silk scarf and don the striking dress. When I emerged from the dressing room, the clerk exclaimed that I looked wonderful in the dress. As I gazed at my reflection in the mirror, I decided I agreed with her.

"It really looks stunning on you," she gushed. "Very flattering. It's versatile, too. I think it works just as well for a special occasion as it does for a casual one."

"Do you really think so?" I asked. She affirmed what I was already thinking: no matter which restaurant Brian chose, this dress would be appropriate for me to wear.

"I really do!"

"All right. I'll take it," I said decisively, before I had a chance to think about how much I was about to spend on a totally unnecessary purchase.

"I'll put it on a hanger for you as soon as you're ready." I thought the hanger was a nice touch. Most shops would have stuffed the dress into a shopping bag.

By the time I stepped to the checkout counter, she had the dress ensconced in a pink plastic bag hanging beside the register. The bag had the shop's logo—a rose—and its name, Desert Rose Boutique, on it.

"Cash or charge?"

I handed her my debit card. I knew my credit card was close to its limit, and, after my grocery shopping spree, I didn't have enough cash left to pay for the pricey dress. The transaction seemed to take forever to process. I began to feel nervous, wondering if the bank had put a hold on Brian's check, but, if so, they certainly hadn't informed me.

"Ah. Here we are," the clerk said, as she ripped the receipt from the cash register. "Sorry that took so long."

A jingling bell signaled the opening of the front door. I hoped it was Jill, returning from the bank. Now would be a perfect time to speak with her, since there were no other customers in the boutique. As soon as I saw her, I had no doubt that she was Ulysses's ex-wife.

"This lady's been waiting to see you," the redhead told her boss.

I was prepared with my business card and brochures, and, since I was wearing one of my own dyed scarves, I had a sample handy to show her. She listened to my spiel politely and asked about wholesale terms.

"Let me show you the wooden display stand that I have available. It's free with an initial order of a dozen scarves."

"All right," she agreed. She definitely took notice when I reached for the dress I'd bought and folded it over my arm. The fact that I'd made a purchase at her store couldn't hurt, I thought, although I doubted that she'd buy my scarves solely because I'd bought a dress from her shop.

When I returned with the display, she looked it over with a skeptical eye. "It's very nice," she said, "but I don't really have enough counter space for it. Would you consider giving me a discount with my first order, instead?"

I never would have thought to ask for a different perk on an opening order, just as I never would have made a sale as handily as the redheaded clerk, who'd made the whole process appear seamless. What she was asking for wasn't unreasonable, so I had to come up with an answer fast.

"How about a ten-percent discount off wholesale?" I suggested.

"Make it fifteen, and we have a deal."

I was tempted to say "twelve and a half," but I didn't want to lose the sale, and I could tell that she could be a tough negotiator. Besides, she had more experience at this than I did.

"Done." I wrote up the order for a dozen scarves, and she gave me a check to pay for half the amount of the invoice, just as my terms specified. I was a little surprised that she hadn't tried to get me to agree to bill her with a thirty-day grace period, but perhaps she sensed I couldn't afford to do that. She definitely had me pegged as a rookie, though.

I'd made a sale, but I hadn't accomplished my main mission. I needed to get Jill to talk, but our business was essentially concluded. I should have tried to chat with her before going into my sales pitch, but, luckily, Jill provided me an opening herself.

"I see you're from Lonesome Valley," she said, glancing at my business card. "My daughter lives there, too."

I didn't want to appear too eager, even though I couldn't wait to learn more details.

"Yes, it's a wonderful town," I said. "I moved there after my divorce," I added, hoping that our having something in common might encourage her to talk to me,

"Ah" was her only response.

"How does your daughter like Lonesome Valley?"

"It may be a little tame for her. I think Samantha would prefer a big city, but she was offered a good job at Lonesome Valley Hospital, and she didn't want to turn it down."

Bingo! She'd told me exactly what I wanted to know.

"The hospital gift shop is one of my accounts," I told her. Of course, it was my only other account besides hers, but she didn't need to know that.

"Well, I hope you're not planning to saturate the market with your scarves. I like to keep my merchandise unique. I don't want my customers seeing the same thing in other places around town."

"No problem," I said. "You'll be the exclusive retailer in Sedona." I knew there was no way I could keep up with lots of scarf accounts and still have time for my painting. I figured by the time I added a few more accounts in Lonesome Valley and perhaps Prescott or Phoenix, I'd have more than enough dyeing to do.

"I appreciate it," she told me. "Oh, and by the way, you are going to give me free shipping on my first order, aren't you?"

Chapter 34

Skunked again! It was time to leave the Desert Rose Boutique before I ended up paying *Jill* to sell my scarves. After agreeing to her last request, I hastily exited the shop. I could have kicked myself for giving in to all her demands, but, at least, I'd learned what I'd come for. Jill had given me her business card along with her check when she'd paid me the deposit on her initial wholesale order. I hadn't looked at it at the time, but now I glanced at the card and saw that she was going by the name Beth Applegate. She'd ditched Jill Durand somewhere along the way. Perhaps she'd remarried or maybe she'd resumed using her maiden name. Whatever the case, I'd learned two very important things: Jill Durand lived in Sedona, only an hour's drive from Lonesome Valley, and her daughter Samantha worked at the Lonesome Valley Hospital. Given that Lieutenant Belmont thought nurse Samantha looked so much like Jill that he'd momentarily mistaken her for Jill, I had no doubt that the nurse and Samantha Applegate were one and the same.

I left the Desert Rose Boutique and headed toward the Sedona city limits. I pulled off the road, into a parking lot, and made three calls before continuing on my way. I kept each brief, since I was in a hurry to get home now that I'd found out what I'd come to Sedona for.

After giving Belle the scoop, I let her know I should be home soon, so she wouldn't have to check on Laddie again. Dave Martinez was out of the office when I called the police station, so I left a short message on his voice mail, telling him that Jill Durand, aka Beth Applegate, lived in Sedona. The last call to Lieutenant Belmont woke the grumpy detective from a nap.

"Yeah?"

"It's Amanda Trent. I have news."

"I have news for you, too," he said smugly. "That nurse Samantha—her last name is—"

"Applegate," we both said at the same time.

"She's Jill's daughter," I told him. "Jill's still living in Sedona. She goes by the name Beth Applegate."

"Well, Ms. Snoop, I guess you're proud of yourself," he said sarcastically.

"Give me a break. You wanted to know, didn't you?"

"Yeah, yeah. Good work," he said grudgingly.

"Thanks." I never thought I'd hear anything close to a compliment from him. "Now do you think you can find out whether or not she's Ulysses's daughter? I know she won't be back on duty until Friday, but you could talk to her then."

"I'll talk to her, all right."

"Talk, not interrogate."

"I know what I'm doing. Count on it." With that, he hung up. I suppose I shouldn't have impugned his questioning tactics, but having been on the receiving end of them myself a couple if times, I knew how abrasive he could be. The old saying "catch more flies with honey than with vinegar" wasn't something the lieutenant practiced usually, but if he could bring himself to play up the helpless patient persona, rather than the rude detective, I had a feeling he'd get a lot farther.

Since there was little traffic and I didn't encounter another motor home on my drive back to Lonesome Valley, I arrived home with hours to spare before my date with Brian.

After pacifying my pets, who made a big fuss over me when I came in the door, I spent a few hours in the studio, working on my painting of Toby, the bloodhound with the soulful big brown eyes. While I worked, I alternately thought of my dress purchase and worried that I shouldn't have splurged on it and thought about the ramifications of my discovery that Jill lived nearby and that Samantha, her daughter, worked at Lonesome Valley Hospital, where Ulysses had been murdered. I kept cautioning myself that such a coincidence did not mean that Samantha had strangled Ulysses. There was still a lot to learn about her. On the other hand, she was certainly shaping up as a prime suspect, as far as I was concerned.

After a while, it was time to get ready for my dinner date. I fussed with my hair and applied more makeup than I usually wore, but I didn't do a very good job of it. My eyeliner looked squiggly, and my mascara had clumped on my lashes, so I had to start over. As I painstakingly applied my eye makeup for the second time, Laddie sat in the bathroom doorway, his head cocked to one side, watching my progress. He obviously sensed that something was up, and even Mona Lisa paid attention. When I slipped on my new maxi dress, she swished around my ankles, meowing loudly. I was about to pick her up when the doorbell rang and she scurried away to hide under the bed.

"Here goes nothing," I told Laddie, as he waited eagerly at the front door for me to open it. I had to admit I felt a little bit nervous, even though I kept telling myself not to be ridiculous, but the fact was I hadn't been on a date with anyone except Ned in decades.

I opened the door, and Laddie rushed forward before I could slow him down. Luckily, Brian didn't seem to mind, and he scratched my friendly retriever behind the ears. When he looked up, he became tongue-tied and stared at me for what seemed like a very long time, although it was probably only a few seconds.

"You look so beautiful this evening," he said, and then thought twice about his declaration. "I mean you *always* look beautiful, but you look especially beautiful in that dress."

"Thank you," I said, hoping to put the poor man out of his misery. He'd turned red as he spoke. "And you look very handsome yourself." I wasn't fibbing. In his sports coat and slacks, Brian cut a rather dashing figure, but he turned even redder at my comment.

I grabbed my small silver clutch, told Laddie to be a good boy, and we were off.

"I made a reservation at Mon Ami at the resort. I hope that's all right," he said, as soon as we were in his car.

"Of course. That sounds good." I'd never ventured there on my own, since it was the most expensive restaurant in town.

Brian didn't say much on the drive to the resort. I made small talk, and he responded mostly with nods and short comments. He hadn't been at all reticent when we'd walked Laddie the evening before, but he was clearly ill at ease, and my attempts to draw him out hadn't worked too well so far. If this kept up during dinner, it was going to be a very long evening.

When Brian pulled up under the resort's portico, the designated drop-off for valet parking, a young man in a resort uniform immediately opened my door for me while Brian took a receipt from another valet.

"It's this way," he said, as he steered me to the right, down a long hallway and across a courtyard. "Shortcut," he grinned as we left the courtyard and came out next to the restaurant.

"This place is so huge," I said. "I only know my way around the mall."

"You've been here before?"

"A few times to the art gallery and frame shop and once my son and I had lunch at Cabo." I didn't mention the time Brooks had urgently called me to deliver Olivia's ransom and I'd gone to Ulysses's suite to pick it up.

I noticed that only half the tables were occupied, as the maître'd escorted us to our table and pulled a chair out to seat me. Seconds later, our server appeared with a wine list.

I was about to look at it when I noticed Brooks and Olivia tucked away at a quiet table in the corner.

"Would you please excuse me for a minute, Brian? That lady over there lost her husband a few days ago, and I'd like to give her my condolences."

"Sure," he said, standing as I got up.

Brooks and Olivia looked up in surprise as I appeared at their table.

"Olivia, I wanted to tell you how sorry I am."

"Thank you, Amanda. It's been very difficult having to stay here while the police sort things out. I should be back in Santa Fe, making arrangements for Ulysses's memorial service and settling his estate, but, instead, I'm stuck here."

Brooks frowned, and Olivia immediately backtracked.

"I don't mean to disparage your hospitality, Brooks. You've been more than generous, allowing me to stay here, and you did so much for Ulysses." Her voice broke, and a tear trickled down her cheek, but she swiped it away. "There's so much to do."

"I'm sure it won't be long. I can check with the coroner's office and Sergeant Martinez again in the morning, if you'd like," Brooks offered.

"I should get back," I murmured, sensing my timing wasn't ideal. "Again, I'm very sorry for your loss."

Although the encounter had been awkward, I'd felt the need to convey my condolences personally, because the opportunity had presented itself, especially since I hadn't yet sent Olivia a sympathy card; in fact, I hadn't purchased one yet.

When I returned to our table, Brian smiled at me, stood up, and pulled my chair out for me. As dinner progressed, Brian relaxed, and we had a pleasant conversation over excellent food. He told me some funny stories about incidents that had happened on the oil rig, and I began to get more of a sense of the man. When he finally confessed that this was his first date in years and I countered that it was my first in decades, we had a good laugh together.

It wasn't until Brian walked me to the front door at the end of the evening that things turned awkward again.

"Thank you for a lovely evening," I said.

Brian moved closer, leaning toward me.

"Hey, neighbors!"

Chapter 35

Dennis's hearty greeting startled both of us, and Brian jerked back, looking around for Dennis. He was coming up the walk, carrying a metal case.

"I was on my way over to show you my new socket wrench set," Dennis told Brian. "I got a great deal on it."

"I'll leave you two to it," I said, unlocking my front door. I could hear Mona Lisa yowling and Laddie, who seldom barked, emitted a deep "woof." "It sounds as though my furry friends are getting restless." I smiled and thanked Brian again before easing the door closed.

I'd have been willing to bet Brian had been leaning in for a kiss when Dennis interrupted us, and maybe it was just as well he had shown up when he had. I still didn't know whether I was ready for a man in my life. Unlike Chip, who took romance lightly, Brian was the serious type, or, at least, I thought he was, and I didn't want to lead him on, but I didn't want to rule him out, either. Perhaps I was the one who was overthinking the situation, though. We'd had a lovely evening, once Brian had gotten over his nervousness.

Laddie whined softly and looked up at me.

"Don't worry, Laddie," I said, giving him a hug. "You're my best boy."

He snuggled closer for another cuddle and succeeded in getting it before Mona Lisa jumped down from her kitty tree to join us, pouncing on my feet and ignoring Laddie, who backed up to make room for her.

As I hung the aubergine dress in my tiny closet, pushing other clothes aside so that the pricey dress wouldn't be pinned between them, I decided my purchase had been worth it, but I didn't plan on more splurges anytime soon.

After I went to bed, I mentally reviewed my to-do list for the next day. I'd get up early and take Laddie for a walk before my scheduled half-day at the Roadrunner began at nine. After that, I'd have the rest of the day free to paint. Before I fell asleep, I wondered whether Lieutenant Belmont would have any success finding out whether Samantha was Ulysses's daughter. Now that I'd learned that Samantha was Jill's daughter, I figured a public records search for her birth certificate was in order, but Sergeant Martinez might have better luck on that score than I would. My last thought before I drifted off to sleep was that Dave Martinez hadn't returned my phone call. I added contacting him to my unwritten to-do list and promptly fell asleep.

The following morning, I was waiting for a keyholder to come along and open the door to the Roadrunner when a car slid into one of the parking spaces directly in front of the gallery. The driver jumped out, and I could see that it was Pamela's husband Rich. He went around the car to the other side, opened the passenger door for Pamela, and offered her his arm when she got out. She clung to him, as I'd seen her do a couple of other times, and didn't let go until she had to get the key out of her purse. Rich took it, unlocked the door, and held it open for us.

"I hope you weren't waiting too long," Pamela said.

"Just a few minutes."

"Tiffany called me at home just before we left. She's sick today and won't be coming in this morning, so it will be just the two of us."

"Thursday mornings aren't usually too busy."

"That's what I thought, too. I didn't think I needed to call someone else in," Pamela said, turning on the lights.

"Ladies, why don't I run next door and get you some coffee while you're getting set up," Rich volunteered.

"That would be wonderful," Pamela agreed. "Amanda, what would you like?"

After I decided on a mocha and Pamela said she'd have the same, Rich left, whistling on his way.

"He seems happy," I commented.

"You mean happier than the last time you saw him here?"

"Well, yes."

"Things have settled down, but I'm not sure it's over yet. He hasn't been raging, but he's acting possessive. I can hardly go outside to get a breath of fresh air by myself. It's a big change from a few months ago when he was seldom home, and I have to admit I'm flattered that he's paying so much attention to me again, but sometimes it's a bit much. And, of course, I don't dare mention Chip's name or call him about Roadrunner business for fear that Rich will object. It's probably just as well Chip's not using the apartment upstairs anymore and has resigned from the board. Otherwise, I might never be able to set foot in the Roadrunner again."

By the time Rich returned with our mochas and a regular cup of coffee for himself, we'd prepared the register, dusted the gallery, and cleaned the glass on the jewelry counter.

"Thank you for the mocha, Rich," I said. "Why don't you and Pamela take yours back to the office? I'll keep an eye on things here."

"We'll do that," Pamela said, "but be sure to call me if you need help."

I had time to take only a couple of sips of my chocolatey drink before our first prospective customer of the day appeared. She spent quite a while wandering around, looking at the artwork, and kept me busy answering her questions, but she left without making a purchase.

I returned to my now-cold mocha and slowly sipped my drink. I heard a muffled tone and scrambled to retrieve my phone from my purse, which I'd deposited in the drawer under the cash register when I'd come in earlier. I located it just in time to take the call.

"Hello."

"Told you so."

Chapter 36

"What? Who is this?" I asked.

"It's Bill Belmont. Our suspect is in custody as we speak." he said smugly.

"Samantha?"

"You got it."

"What happened?"

"Dave Martinez did some records checking and located Samantha's birth certificate. Her mother's name is listed as Jill Elizabeth Durand."

"And her father's name?"

"Ulysses Durand."

"But does she know who her father is?"

"No idea, but Dave intends to find out."

"You say she's in custody?"

"I may have exaggerated. Dave hasn't arrested her yet, but he's taken her in for questioning."

"How did you find out? I thought he wasn't going to discuss the case with you."

"I have my ways. Don't tell Dawn, though, or Dave and I will both be in the doghouse."

"Wow! It's awful to think Ulysses's own daughter may have

murdered him in his hospital bed."

"Gotta go. The vampire's here to take my blood." He hung up.

Perhaps I'd been right about Samantha, but it didn't make me feel good that a daughter—and a nurse, to boot—could do such a terrible thing. I called Belle immediately to let her know what the lieutenant had told me. I knew that part of the reason he'd been willing to share the information was to let me know that the police were perfectly capable of handling the investigation. Subtext: they didn't need *my* help to do it.

When I'd finished my call to Belle, I dropped my phone back into my bag and stooped to put my purse back under the counter. When I stood up, I was surprised to see Brooks standing near the jewelry counter. I hadn't heard anyone come in the door, and I'd had my back turned while I'd talked to Belle. Usually, I kept an eagle eye on the door so that I could greet customers the second they came in, but I'd been so engrossed in my conversation with Belle that I hadn't been paying attention.

"I didn't mean to startle you, Amanda," Brooks began, "but I confess I overheard that the police may have found who killed Ulysses."

"It's possible. I understand they're questioning her now. She's a nurse at the hospital here."

"Why would a nurse do such a thing? Ulysses was getting better. It can't have been a mercy killing."

"Nobody knows for sure, but she's Ulysses's daughter. Goes by the name of Samantha Applegate. It's possible Ulysses may not have known it, either. His first wife must have been pregnant when she left him, but she may not have told him. That's all speculation, by the way."

"Unbelievable!" he said, hoisting a large shopping bag and placing it on the counter next to the cash register. "And here's something else that's unbelievable. I need you to tell me if you recognize this." He tipped the shopping bag on its side, reached in, and pulled out a gym bag with the Lonesome Valley Resort logo on its side.

"Yes, it's like the one you gave me to deliver the ransom money, but aren't all the bags alike?"

He flipped one of the handles down so that we could examine it. "Anything?" he prodded.

"Well, yes: that jagged white scuff mark there, on the handle. That's the same bag! Where did you get it?"

"I found it stuffed in the back of Gabrielle's closet. She used to go to the gym at the resort all the time, so, at first, I didn't think anything of it, but then I took a second look. I remembered the mark on the handle. My own wife's a kidnapper!"

"Why would she do something like that?"

"Money. Why else? I bet she was already planning to divorce me, and she wanted a stake before she went back to New York. She signed a pre-nup when we got married, so she knew she wouldn't get much from me."

"She must have had help, Brooks. She couldn't possibly have pulled it off alone. Remember the call Ulysses got from the kidnapper at the art auction? Gabrielle was right there in the room, and she wasn't on the phone at the time, but she had obviously already contacted her accomplice, or our caller wouldn't have known where we were or who you were with."

"You might be right. It could be that golf instructor at the resort that she's been flirting with. He's so infatuated with her he'd probably do anything she asked. I'm going to find out right now."

"Brooks, no. Let the police handle it. You *are* planning to go to the police, aren't you?"

"Yes, I was on my way to the station, but I wanted to make sure you recognized the bag, too. I suppose you're right," he said with a sigh, "but I'm going to give them his name. They can check him out."

The rest of the morning passed slowly. We had only a handful of visitors to the gallery, and we didn't sell a single thing.

"I hope it picks up this afternoon," I told Pamela before I left. "It's a good thing you didn't call anyone in to substitute for Tiffany."

"I'm sure it will liven up tomorrow, if not today," Pamela said confidently. "It always does."

Pamela was right, of course. Weekends were the busiest time for all the businesses that lined Lonesome Valley's Main Street.

I headed home, determined to work on my portrait of Toby. With luck, I'd be able to complete my work on it in a few more days. Just in time, I thought, since I'd received an email inquiry about another pet portrait before I'd left for the gallery earlier. At this point, I didn't have a firm commitment from the buyer, but she'd sounded very interested, so I sent her some more information and a sample contract to look over. I hoped she'd get back to me soon.

After that, I concentrated on Toby's painting, while Laddie snoozed on his bed. Every once in a while, I'd step back to view what I'd painted from a different perspective. The portrait was coming along nicely.

Laddie jumped up and ran to the studio door, so I knew someone was coming up the walk, but I hadn't heard a thing. I swung open the door, and Belle stepped inside, pausing to pet Laddie.

"I knew you'd be working, so I came around the side of the house," she said. Usually, Belle came to my kitchen door when she visited me.

"What's up? Would you like some coffee?"

"No, thanks, Amanda. I'm in a bit of a rush. I told Dennis I'd meet him at the paint store to pick out our colors. We're going to redecorate all three bedrooms. I came to ask to borrow your red two-quart dish. I'm taking a casserole to our Library Auxiliary lunch meeting tomorrow, and I broke the dish I was planning on using."

"Sure."

"I can get it. I know you're working. Just point me in the right direction."

"It's in the bottom cabinet to the right of the sink, on the first shelf."

The minute Belle left the room, Laddie raced to the door again. This time, it was Brian.

"Amanda, I . . . I wanted to tell you what a good time I had last evening," he said, leaning toward me, much as he had the previous evening.

"Amanda, I can't find it," Belle said, as she came back into the studio.

Brian jumped back as though he'd heard a shot and turned red.

"Oh, hi, Brian," Belle said lightly.

"I'd better go," he said.

"You just got here," Belle protested, but Brian was long gone by the time she got the words out of her mouth.

Chapter 37

"That's strange," she said. "I wonder why he left in such a big hurry. I didn't interrupt anything, did I?"

"No, he just showed up a few seconds ago." I snapped my fingers. "I just remembered. I left my red dish at Ralph's the other night. I'll run by and pick it up as soon as I'm finished here."

"Don't go to any trouble, Amanda."

"It's no trouble, really. I need to pick it up, anyway, and it'll give me the perfect excuse to check on Ralph. I'll bring it over this evening."

"Well, if you're sure. . . ."

"Of course I am. It's no problem. See you later."

After Belle left, I decided I should probably take Ralph something for his dinner tonight. Despite all the groceries now in his larder, I didn't know how much cooking he did. After I put my paints away for the day, I made some cheese and sour cream enchiladas to take to him.

Although I hadn't planned on going out again, my errand shouldn't take too long. I picked up Mona Lisa to give her a cuddle, and when I set her down, she scampered off. Laddie stayed by my side until I inched the kitchen door open and assured him I'd be back soon to spend a quiet evening at home.

This time, I didn't need any help from my GPS genie to find my way to Ralph's house. When I parked in the driveway, I saw that Ralph's garage door was up, but it was what I saw inside that aroused my curiosity. There, parked next to his Lincoln Town Car, was a large black pickup truck, the same type of truck I'd seen near the tennis courts when I'd delivered the ransom. I'd never seen Ralph drive any vehicle other than his Town Car. I reminded myself that there must be loads of similar trucks in town, but this was a dark-colored truck like the witness had reported spotting at the scene of Ulysses's accident.

I couldn't resist the urge to satisfy my curiosity. Passing between the Lincoln and the pickup, I walked to the back of the garage and examined the black truck's bumper. It was scratched, and there was a fair amount of white paint on it. I didn't have time to contemplate my next move, because I could hear Ralph's kitchen door opening. Foolishly, I crouched behind the truck. I didn't know whether Ralph would recognize the car parked in his driveway as mine, but he'd certainly know someone was around.

"Hello?" he called. I watched as he circled my car, walking without any aid from his cane or his walker.

Looking around, I saw that there was a back door to the garage. I crept toward it, turned the handle, and gave it a yank. The door didn't budge.

"Anybody here?" Ralph called.

He sounded closer, and when I peeked around the truck, I could see that he was coming toward me. Desperately, I rattled the door handle again, but it was no use. The door was locked.

"Who's there?"

I didn't have any choice but to show myself at this point.

"Amanda, what are you doing in here?"

"I was just going to look for you in the backyard," I said, "but the door's locked."

He came toward me, and I tried to back away, but the truck was parked so close to the side of the garage that I couldn't get through.

"Come on out, Amanda. I'm not going to hurt you," he said wearily. "I suppose you saw it, didn't you?"

I nodded.

"I guess it's time to come clean," he said. "I almost told the chief right after I heard Ulysses had died. I thought I'd killed him, but when I found out he'd been murdered, I decided to keep my mouth shut."

"Oh, Ralph!" My fleeting fear of him had evaporated. He sounded sincere.

"I'm going to turn myself in, Amanda. I'm going to call the chief right now." True to his word, he pulled his cell phone out of his pocket, made the call, and put it on speaker.

I realized that Ralph was still trying to reassure me that I didn't need to be afraid of him.

I could hear a man's deep voice on the other end and the brief conversation between the two. The chief and Ralph were longtime friends, so I wasn't surprised when the chief told him to wait for him at home, that he'd come over soon.

"OK?" Ralph asked after he returned the phone to his pocket.

"OK," I agreed. "Whatever were you thinking, Ralph?"

"Let's go inside, Amanda. You already know part of the story."

"All right," I agreed. "Oh, wait a minute. I brought you

something." I went to the car and grabbed the tray of enchiladas, but I nearly dropped it when I turned around and Ralph was standing right in back of me!

He held up both hands. "Whoa! I didn't mean to startle you. Let me take that."

I handed him the tray, and we went inside, where he set it on the counter. I noticed he was still walking normally. There was no cane or walker in sight.

"Your arthritis must be better," I commented.

"Not better. It never goes away, but the pain has. My doctor started me on some new meds."

I felt a bit ashamed that I'd suspected him of faking the effects of his debilitating arthritis when he'd caught me in the garage and I'd noticed he wasn't having any difficulty walking.

"Were you in on the kidnapping, too?"

"What are you talking about?" he asked.

"Olivia was kidnapped. That's the reason Ulysses was out driving that night. He was on his way to pick her up after the ransom was paid."

"I didn't know. Maybe if I had, I wouldn't have done what I did. No. I'm afraid I followed Ulysses on the spur of the moment. I happened to be at the resort for dinner that evening, and I saw him leaving the parking area just as the valet brought my truck around. I don't know what I had in mind when I started after him, but I followed him. Then, I took it into my head to give him a scare. I figured it would serve him right for ripping off my painting and then acting as though we were buddies when I came to his show at Brooks's new gallery. Did he honestly think I was so stupid that I didn't know what he'd done? Anyway, I miscalculated when I came up behind him. I wasn't trying to hit his car, but I stepped on the gas too hard. You know the rest."

"You should have stopped at the scene."

"I know. What can I say? I panicked. I may be old, but I'm not too wise. When I found out Ulysses was in a coma, I almost called the chief to tell him what I'd done, but, well, I didn't want to spend my last years in prison, even though I deserve it."

I could hardly believe what Ralph had told me, but the white marks on the bumper of his truck certainly confirmed his story, and the painting displayed in his den served as a daily reminder of the wrong Ulysses had done to him.

When the chief arrived, we all sat at Ralph's kitchen table while he repeated his story.

"Ralph, I won't kid you. You're in some trouble here." The chief pulled a card out of his pocket and handed it to Ralph. "Call this guy, and then have him call me. He's the best criminal attorney in town. You're going to need him. We'll arrange for you to turn yourself in sometime tomorrow. If you're lucky, your lawyer can work out a plea deal with the district attorney."

"Will I go to jail?"

"*Call* him."

Chapter 38

I was so shaken by Ralph's unexpected confession that I almost forgot to pick up my red casserole dish that I'd promised to loan Belle. Ralph's mood had remained resolute. He'd called the lawyer, as the chief had suggested, only to be shunted to voice mail, and he had to leave a message. When I left, he was staring at his phone, waiting for the attorney to return his call.

Belle's eyes widened when I told her that Ralph had admitted to causing Ulysses's accident. We talked for a while after I dropped off my red dish and concluded that the mysteries had been solved: Ralph had caused Ulysses's auto accident; Gabrielle had been behind Olivia's kidnapping; Samantha had strangled her own father.

"Get some rest," Belle urged me, as I got up to go home. "You look tired."

"I will. It's been a long day. I'm still having trouble wrapping my mind around Ralph as a hit-and-run driver. I wonder what will happen to him."

"If his lawyer's as good as the chief said, maybe he'll avoid prison."

I wondered about that myself, as I tossed and turned for most of the night. Ralph said he hadn't intended to bump

Ulysses's car, but his driving had been reckless and he'd left the scene of the accident he'd caused.

Sometime during the night, I finally drifted off. The next morning, I was shocked to see that it was a few minutes after seven when Laddie and Mona Lisa both piled on me. I'd been dimly aware that they were after me to get up for several minutes, but I'd kept my eyes closed and played possum while Laddie had nudged me, and Mona Lisa had batted at my right arm.

"OK, you win," I said sleepily, as I rolled out of bed. Feeling groggy, I put the kettle on and filled their bowls while I waited for the water to boil. I definitely needed a strong pot of tea to kick-start my day, but I didn't have a chance to take a sip before my phone rang.

"Guess who's on duty." This time, I recognized Lieutenant Belmont's voice.

"You mean—?"

"Yeah, that nurse Samantha. She's here. You have to find out what's going on. I can't get a hold of Dave. He didn't come with Dawn to visit me last night, and he's not answering my calls."

"What makes you think he'll tell me anything?'

"You put him onto her in the first place."

"I suppose I could ask him, but he may not want to tell me."

"Oh, he'll tell you, all right. You have a way of worming information out of people."

"I'm not sure about that. Anyway, I need to wake up before I do anything."

"Well, get with it. I've been awake for hours," he grumbled. He hung up before I could respond.

I took my time drinking my tea and puttering around the

house. Laddie was begging to go for a walk, but I was still in my robe. I took him out to the backyard for a game of fetch instead. After a while, I realized I was deliberately stalling. I was just as curious as Lieutenant Belmont to know why Dave had released Samantha. However, I didn't have the same confidence as the lieutenant did that Dave would share that information with me. Besides, I still felt a bit fuzzy headed. I took a shower, hoping it might help me revive. Afterward, I felt more alert. I dressed and went to the kitchen to brew another pot of tea.

I was turning the burner on when Dave called me himself, asking me if I could come to the station to formally identify the gym bag that Brooks had turned in. I told him I'd be there in a few minutes, but I didn't ask him about Samantha, reasoning that he might be more likely to tell me why she was back at work if I asked him in person.

Brooks was coming out of the station as I was going in. He told me he'd signed a statement identifying the gym bag as the same bag we'd used to deliver the ransom money. "This has been a terrible week," he told me. "Ulysses's death, then finding out Gabrielle wants a divorce, and learning that she's a kidnapper." He sounded dejected, and no wonder. Not only had his wife left him, but she'd also turned out to be a criminal. "Well, I'd better get back to the resort and see whether Olivia needs any help. She's going back to Santa Fe this afternoon to arrange for the memorial now that the coroner's released Ulysses's body."

Dave Martinez was waiting for me at the reception area inside the station.

"Hello, Amanda." He lifted the gym bag onto the counter between us. "Look familiar?"

"They all look alike, but the one I used had a white scuff mark on the inside of the handle. There." I pointed to the mark.

"You're sure this is the same bag, then?"

"I'm sure. I remember the shape of the mark, because it kind of looks like a lightning bolt."

"Oh, yeah; I see. I need you to sign a statement confirming your identification."

"Sure."

"This will just take a second." He quickly typed the statement, printed it, and handed it to me.

"Here you are," I said, after I read it and signed on the dotted line. "Say, Dave, I was wondering about Samantha." I tried to sound nonchalant, although I wasn't sure I'd pulled it off.

He didn't seem to notice my effort to appear casual, though.

"Iron-clad alibi for the time of the murder. She was involved in a fender bender on her way to work on the morning Ulysses was killed. Mike Dyson went to the scene and wrote the report. She didn't do it, and neither did her mother. Jill, or Beth as she calls herself now, was in Sedona at some breakfast meeting when Ulysses was strangled. She has about thirty witnesses to vouch for her. We're going to have to look elsewhere for the killer."

"I'm glad they weren't involved," I said. "They sure seemed like good suspects, though."

Evidently, I'd been too hasty to believe that Ulysses's murder had been solved. As I drove away from the police station, it occurred to me that, if Samantha hadn't known that Ulysses was her father, she must know by now, after all the police questioning.

In everything I'd ever read about Ulysses—and I'd read a considerable amount since Brooks had first announced that

Ulysses would be the featured artist in his new gallery's first show—there had never been any mention of Ulysses's having children. In fact, one article praised the artist for his generous contributions to a children's charity "despite having no children of his own."

If I'd been Samantha, I'd have been tempted to take the day off, but Lieutenant Belmont had told me she was on duty. I was thinking about how the innocent nurse had been a victim, too, although not as great a victim as her father. Samantha was alive and well, and her father was not.

Suddenly, it hit me! I pulled over to the curb, grabbed my cell phone, and did a quick Internet search, which confirmed my fears.

There was just one more piece of the puzzle to fit into place.

Chapter 39

"Remember yesterday, when I told you Ulysses had a daughter?"

"How could I forget *that* bombshell?" Brooks said. "She's the main suspect in his murder, isn't she?"

"Not anymore. She has an airtight alibi, according to the police. Did you mention he has a daughter to anyone else?"

"I told Olivia. I thought she'd want to know that the police had a suspect."

"So she knows Ulysses has a daughter?"

"She does now. I think it came as a shock to her."

"Brooks, this is important. Could you please make sure Olivia doesn't leave the resort?"

"Why, Amanda? What's going on?"

"I don't have time to explain right now. Please, Brooks!"

"All right."

My hands trembled as I called the police station. When I asked for Dave Martinez, I was unceremoniously cut off and put through to his voice mail. I left a message, before immediately calling Lieutenant Belmont.

He answered my call with a question: "Find out anything?"

"Yes. Listen. Nurse Samantha may be in danger! Can you

get her to come to your room and stay there?"

I expected an argument or a demand for an explanation, but I didn't get one. Instead, the lieutenant snapped "on it" and hung up.

I worked myself into a state of near panic as I sped toward the hospital. Frustratingly, I had to park a block away, and I was breathless from running by the time I entered the lobby, where I planned to ask the receptionist to put me in touch with the hospital's security supervisor. There was a line at the reception center, though, and I didn't think I dared wait.

I did have to wait for the elevator. What seemed like a maddeningly long time was very likely only a few seconds, as I forced myself to stay put, knowing it would take me less time to go upstairs in the elevator than it would for me to climb the stairs when I already felt winded from running from my car to the hospital.

When the lift arrived, I jumped inside and pushed the button for the fourth floor before an approaching couple could reach the elevator.

"Sorry," I called, as the door slid shut. "Emergency!"

As I stepped off, on the fourth floor, my phone rang. I glanced at it. "Brooks?"

"Sorry, Amanda. I can't find Olivia, and she's not answering her phone. It's possible she's here in the resort somewhere, but she's not in her room or any of the restaurants. I'll keep trying to locate her if you want me to."

"Yes, please. I have to go, but I'll explain later."

The nursing station was deserted, as was the hallway, except for an aide who was collecting breakfast trays.

I rushed to Lieutenant Belmont's room and found him sitting up in bed, demanding that Samantha check the bedside monitor.

"There's nothing wrong with the monitor," she announced.

"Are you sure? It keeps making a beeping noise. How's a guy supposed to get any sleep around here with that annoying racket?"

I could tell from her tone that she was tiring of trying to pacify the lieutenant.

"I'll check it again." She looked over the instrument and pronounced it sound. "It's fine. I don't hear any beeping. I do have other patients to check, you know."

When she started toward the door, I moved into her path. "Wait a minute, please, Samantha."

"Yes, wait a minute." The voice came from behind me, and I didn't need to turn around to know it was Olivia. She closed the door and swung back around to face us again, a gun in her hand.

Samantha and I backed away from her, toward the lieutenant's hospital bed.

"Olivia Durand, you're under arrest for the murder of Ulysses Durand. You have the right to—"

"Oh, save it. Who do you think you are, anyway?"

"Lieutenant William Belmont, Lonesome Valley Police Department, and you're under arrest."

"Oh, great, a cop." Olivia sneered, tightening her grip on the pistol.

I assumed she hadn't banked on having to deal with a police officer when she'd tracked down Samantha. Unfortunately, the officer in question was also a post-op patient currently confined to a hospital bed.

Olivia looked at Samantha and gestured with her gun. "You move over there." She indicated the side of the bed where Samantha had been checking the heart monitor earlier.

Samantha, frozen in place, looked absolutely terrified.

When she didn't budge, Olivia repeated, "Move!"

This time, Samantha complied.

"Give it up, Olivia," I said. "You can't very well shoot three people and expect to get away with it."

"Shut up, Mrs. Snoop. Why are you here, anyway? You're always hanging around where you're not wanted."

I ignored that comment and tried to reason with her. "You might as well give yourself up, Olivia. I've alerted the police about you."

"What? *This* old guy? He's not very likely to cause me any trouble."

Lieutenant Belmont glowered at her.

"Why are you doing this?" Samantha whimpered.

"You're a threat to her, Samantha," I said.

"But I don't even know who she is."

"I'm Ulysses's wife," Olivia volunteered. "He never bothered to tell me he had a kid, and you're in my way."

"No, I'm not," Samantha protested. "I didn't know he was my father until yesterday. I haven't done anything to you."

"Not yet, you haven't, and you're not going to, either. Ulysses's estate belongs to me, not some daughter he never knew he had."

I could see that the full effect of Olivia's words were sinking in, and Samantha looked even more frightened than she had before.

"Get over there, and get the cop out of bed," Olivia directed, as she moved closer to Samantha.

I was on the opposite side of the bed, so, even though Olivia's attention wasn't focused on me, there wasn't much I could do to stop her. She kept swinging the gun from side to

PAULA DARNELL

side, alternately training it on Samantha, the lieutenant, and me.

Samantha lowered the rail of the hospital bed, and Lieutenant Belmont tried to steady himself as his feet hit the floor, but, when he stood, he wobbled. Samantha braced him, and he managed to stay on his feet.

"Now, there's going to be an unfortunate accident in the shower." Olivia glanced at me. "I'll take care of *you* later."

In the split second that Olivia slightly diverted her attention, the lieutenant sprang forward and tackled her, but she got a shot off before they both landed on the floor, and the lieutenant cried out in pain.

Samantha looked stunned. I yelled at her to grab the gun and scrambled to move around the bed. Olivia was starting to sit up when Samantha kicked the gun out of her hand while the lieutenant lay groaning on the floor.

Olivia was back on her feet before I reached her. I grabbed her and as we struggled, I feared I wouldn't be able to overpower her. She yanked my arm and wrenched it so hard I screamed in pain.

The lieutenant reached out and pulled her ankle. She went down again. This time, she stayed down.

"Give me the gun," the lieutenant croaked. I rushed to pick it up, but my right wrist hurt so much I had to lift it with my left hand before handing it to him.

He leveled it squarely at Olivia and repeated, "Olivia Durand, you're under arrest for the murder of Ulysses Durand." He continued until he'd informed her of her rights. Then, he told Samantha, "Call 9-1-1, and make it snappy."

While Samantha made the emergency call from the lieutenant's bedside phone, both he and Olivia remained on the floor, although the lieutenant was sitting up by this time and Olivia had complied with his order to lie prone with her arms behind her neck, fingers interlaced.

A hospital security team burst into the room, followed, a few minutes later, by several police officers led by Sergeant Martinez.

Dave Martinez took one look at the scene and another close look at his wounded colleague, who was still sitting on the floor with Olivia's own gun trained on her.

"We'll take it from here, Bill. Help the lieutenant get up," he directed Mike Dyson, while the other two officers handcuffed Olivia and led her away. Supported by Mike, the lieutenant hopped toward the bed, his foot dripping blood all the way, and sat on the edge.

Still shaking from her ordeal, Samantha stood quietly in the corner, but, as soon as she saw that Lieutenant Belmont's foot was injured, she rushed to his side.

In the blur of activity, I didn't realize I was holding my throbbing right wrist with my left hand. I could barely move my arm; it hurt so much.

"Amanda, are you all right?" Dave Martinez asked.

"Olivia wrenched my arm. You wouldn't believe how strong she is."

"Strong enough to strangle her husband," the lieutenant confirmed. "Dyson, get a move on, and take Mrs. Trent to the emergency room."

Chapter 40

"Thanks for the lift, Mike," I said, as he steered his patrol car to the curb in front of my house.

"No problem, Amanda. If you like, I can drop your car off here after work. With your arm in a sling, you're not going to be doing a lot of driving for a few days."

"That's true, but there's no need. I'm sure my neighbors will go pick it up for me."

"OK. Hold on, Amanda. Let me come around to open your door. You can't very well open it with your arm like that."

Mike jumped out, came around to the passenger side, and opened the door for me. Moving awkwardly, I got out of the police car and saw Brian rushing toward us.

"Amanda, let me help. It looks like you've been in an accident."

"Take care, Amanda," Mike said, as he hopped back into his patrol car. "Gotta get back."

Automatically, I started to lift my right arm to wave, but the searing pain quickly reminded me not to move it.

"Keys?"

I eased my purse off my left shoulder and handed it to Brian. "In my bag. Would you mind digging them out?"

After some rummaging, Brian found the keys, and we went into my house to be greeted by a desperate Laddie, while Mona Lisa hopped up on her kitty tree to observe us from on high.

"Could you please let Laddie out, Brian?"

"Sure. Come on, boy." He patted his leg, as I pointed him toward the door.

"And stay with him?" Brian looked at me, his eyebrows raised. "Just to be on the safe side. Coyotes: it's not likely they'd bother him, but you never know."

"Oh, sure. I should have realized."

I settled myself on the sofa, relieved to be back in my cozy home.

When they came back in, Laddie settled himself by my side, and I draped my left arm around him, while Brian sat in the chair opposite.

"I suppose you're wondering what happened," I said.

"I sure am."

"It's a long story."

"I'm all ears."

"It all started when I received an invitation to go to the very first show at the new art gallery at the resort. . . ."

As I told my story, Brian listened without interruption. When I finished, he asked, "All this has been going on since I moved here?"

I nodded.

"I had no idea. No wonder you seemed distracted. I'm totally in awe of you. You really are the most amazing woman!"

"You think I'm amazing?"

He stood and leaned down toward me. "And how!" he said, planting a gentle kiss on my lips.

* * *

A few weeks after Brian had met me as I returned from the emergency room, Belle, Dennis, and I were enjoying a barbecue on their patio, while the dogs frolicked in the backyard, running over to us from time to time to beg for a tidbit.

"Hear anything from Brian lately?" Dennis asked slyly.

"You know I have." Brian was back at work on the rig, and, although he wasn't able to phone, he'd sent me several emails.

Dennis winked at me.

"You two make a cute couple," Belle said.

"Well, let's not get ahead of ourselves. We're going to take it slow."

"Uh huh."

"Belle! I mean it."

"I know you do. Just kidding. So what's the latest on the crime front? We haven't seen you all week."

Belle and Dennis had taken a short vacation to see the sights in the Four Corners area with a stop at the Grand Canyon on the way home.

"Not by her own choice, but Gabrielle's back, and she's claiming that Olivia staged her own kidnapping. She says Olivia left the gym bag—the one I identified for Sergeant Martinez—in Gabrielle's car and all she herself did was bring it home. Of course, her story doesn't hold up. I'm sure she contacted Olivia from the art auction, right before Ulysses got that call from the kidnapper. He was talking to his own wife—well, maybe; I'll get to that later—but he didn't recognize her voice, because she was using some device to distort it. By the way, the police found several packets of money when they searched her suitcases."

"Sounds like they split the ransom," Dennis said.

"It's strange that Olivia staged her own kidnapping and then murdered her husband. If she was after his money, why bother with the kidnapping in the first place?" Belle added.

"I don't think she planned to kill him at first," I said. "If Ralph hadn't come along and caused the accident, maybe she never would have decided to do it, but, when Ulysses was in a coma, I really think she expected him to die, leaving her a rich widow, and maybe she figured that millions were better than hundreds of thousands. He threw her a curve when he woke up."

"So it was all about the money?"

"With a side of self-justification, because both Olivia and Gabrielle had convinced themselves that their husbands didn't appreciate them. Oh, and here's another crazy fact: Ulysses never did divorce Jill, so it turns out that Olivia wasn't legally married to Ulysses, anyway. Ulysses didn't have a will, but Olivia was counting on that to work in her favor. As Ulysses's surviving spouse, she would have inherited his entire estate if he had no children."

"So, when she found out he had a daughter, Samantha had to go, I suppose," Dennis said.

"As Ulysses's daughter, she stands to inherit three-fourths of his estate. That would have left Olivia with a mere one-quarter, which evidently wasn't enough for her. She wanted it all. Of course, at the time, she didn't know that she and Ulysses weren't legally married. Since she wasn't his wife, it turns out she wasn't his heir, either. Since he never divorced Jill, she may be in line to receive an inheritance, too.

I feel bad for suspecting Samantha of strangling Ulysses. Jill didn't tell her Ulysses was her father until after he was murdered. She probably never would have told Samantha if the police hadn't questioned them both."

"Poor Samantha! It had to be a lot to take in," Belle commented.

"Yes, but I think she'll be able to cope. She was back at work the day after she found out. It may be what saved her. If she'd been alone when Olivia found her, the outcome might have been very different. It took all three of us to subdue her."

"I still can't say I like Bill Belmont," Dennis said. "I've never been a fan of his, but I give him credit for taking her down. You, too, Amanda. It's a good thing you figured it out when you did."

"When I saw you with that sling on your arm, my heart sank, I can tell you," Belle said. "I knew you'd be worried you wouldn't be able to paint."

"I was lucky I only had to wear it for a few days."

"Is your wrist still bothering you?"

"Not too much. I can paint as long as I don't work for too long at a time. I was finally able to finish that pet portrait of Toby, the bloodhound."

"That's great, Amanda! I'm so happy things are getting back to normal," Belle said, as she cut us each a slice of coconut cake. "Aren't you glad you moved to Lonesome Valley?"

"I really am," I said with a smile, "but I have to admit I thought it would be a wee bit quieter here."

We laughed at that, while Laddie and Mr. Big joined in, wagging their tails and yipping with joy as they raced around us.

Read all about how Amanda unravels a new mystery in *Hemlock for the Holidays*, Book 3 in *A Fine Art Mystery Series*.

Recipes

Cheese and Sour Cream Enchiladas

Amanda made these cheese and sour cream enchiladas for Ralph, who enjoyed having a home-cooked meal that he didn't have to prepare himself.

If you prefer spicier enchiladas, you can add chilies to the filling and top the enchiladas with hot enchilada sauce.

Ingredients

6 eight-inch flour tortillas
1 sixteen-ounce container sour cream
1 ½ cups shredded Monterey Jack cheese
2 ½ cups Cheddar cheese
½ cup chopped green onions
1 ten-ounce can mild red enchilada sauce

Directions

Preheat the oven to 350 degrees.

Reserve one cup shredded Cheddar cheese for the topping. To make the filling, combine sour cream, remaining cheeses, chopped onions, and ¼ cup enchilada sauce in a mixing bowl. Spoon mixture onto each tortilla a bit off center and roll up. Place seam side down in a nonstick, 9" x 13" baking pan. When all six enchiladas are made, spoon the remaining enchilada sauce evenly over the enchiladas and sprinkle the reserved one cup of Cheddar cheese on top.

Bake 35 minutes.

Makes six enchiladas.

Individual, Open-Faced Cheeseburger Quesadillas

Here's a quick meal for one. The recipe can easily be expanded to make more servings simply by multiplying the quantity of each ingredient by the number of quesadillas you want to make.

Ingredients

1 eight-inch flour tortilla
¼ pound 85% lean ground beef
¼ cup chopped onion
½ cup sharp cheddar cheese
1 tablespoon ketchup
dill pickles

Directions

Preheat oven to 350 degrees.

Brown chopped onion and ground beef, breaking up ground beef, and cook until done. Drain on paper towels. Put the ground beef mixture into a small bowl and stir in ketchup. Place the tortilla on a baking sheet and spread the ground beef mixture on the top. Sprinkle with cheese. Bake at 350 degrees for ten minutes.

To serve, cut into quarters and top with dill pickles.

Makes one serving.

Chocolate Mousse

Amanda's quick version of chocolate mousse takes less time to prepare than the traditional French version and tastes just as yummy.

Ingredients

2 cups heavy whipping cream
6 ounces finely chopped dark chocolate
¼ cup sugar
1 teaspoon vanilla

Directions

Chill mixing bowl and beaters in the freezer for an hour. Warm one cup of whipping cream in the top of a double boiler over medium heat or in the microwave (do not boil). Remove from heat or microwave, add chocolate, and stir until chocolate is dissolved. Set aside to cool.

In the chilled mixing bowl, whip the remaining cup of cream, slowly adding sugar and vanilla, until soft peaks form. Remove and reserve one-half cup of the whipped cream, which will be used for the topping. Whip the remaining whipped cream mixture until stiff peaks form. Fold the whipped cream mixture, quickly and gently, into the chocolate and cream mixture. Spoon into four small serving dishes and chill for at least one hour before serving.

Optional: top with chocolate curls or chopped walnuts before serving.

Makes four servings.

Date Cake

Belle's grandmother gave her this recipe decades ago, and it's as yummy as ever, especially with a dollop of whipped cream on top!

Cake Ingredients

1 cup pitted, chopped dates
1 cup boiling water
2 tablespoons butter
1 egg
1 cup sugar
1 ½ cups flour
1 teaspoon baking powder
1 teaspoon baking soda

Topping Ingredients

1 cup pitted, chopped dates
¾ cup water
¼ cup sugar
¼ cup chopped walnuts

Directions

Preheat the oven to 350 degrees.

Add boiling water to one cup chopped dates in a small bowl and set aside. Cream softened or melted butter together with egg and sugar. Add dry ingredients to the creamed mixture. Add date mixture and stir until well blended. Bake for 35 minutes in a buttered 9" x 9" baking pan. Remove from oven and test for doneness by inserting a toothpick in the center. If it comes out clean, the cake is done. If not, return the cake to the oven and bake a few minutes longer. Cool the cake in the pan before making the topping.

Add chopped dates, water, and sugar to a small pan and bring to a boil on medium heat. Reduce heat to low and simmer for five minutes or until thickened, stirring often. Do not overcook. When the mixture has thickened, remove from heat and cool for five minutes. Spread the topping evenly on the cake and sprinkle with the chopped walnuts.

Makes nine servings.

ABOUT THE AUTHOR

Award-winning author Paula Darnell is a former college instructor who has a Bachelor of Arts degree in English from the University of Iowa and a Master of Arts degree in English with a Writing Emphasis from the University of Nevada, Reno. *Vanished into Plein Air* is the second book in her Fine Art Mystery series. She's also the author of the DIY Diva Mystery series and *The Six-Week Solution*, a historical mystery set in Nevada. She resides in Las Vegas with her husband Gary and their Pyrador Rocky.

VISIT HER WEBSITE
pauladarnellauthor.com

Read all about how Amanda unravels a new mystery in *Hemlock for the Holidays*, Book 3 in *A Fine Art Mystery Series.*

CPSIA information can be obtained
at www.ICGtesting.com
Printed in the USA
BVHW031816140321
602513BV00024B/179

9 781887 402200